PURSUIT

PURSUIT

LEWIS B. PATTEN

THORNDIKE
C H I V E R S

This Large Print edition is published by Thorndike Press, Waterville, Maine, USA and by BBC Audiobooks Ltd, Bath, England.

Thorndike Press is an imprint of The Gale Group.

Thorndike is a trademark and used herein under license.

The text of this Large Print edition is unabridged.

Other aspects of the book may vary from the original edition.

Set in 16 pt. Plantin.

LIBRARY OF CONGRESS CATALOGING-IN-PUBLICATION DATA

Patten, Lewis B.
  Pursuit / by Lewis B. Patten.
    p. cm. — (Thorndike Press large print western)
  ISBN-13: 978-0-7862-9953-9 (lg. print : alk. paper)
  ISBN-10: 0-7862-9953-3 (lg. print : alk. paper)
  1. Large type books. I. Title.
PS3566.A79P86 2007
813'.54—dc22   2007030752

BRITISH LIBRARY CATALOGUING-IN-PUBLICATION DATA AVAILABLE

Published in 2007 in the U.S. by arrangement with Golden West
Literary Agency.
Published in 2008 in the U.K. by arrangement with Golden West Literary Agency.

U.K. Hardcover: 978 1 405 64358 0 (Chivers Large Print)
U.K. Softcover: 978 1 405 64359 7 (Camden Large Print)

Printed in the United States of America on permanent paper
10 9 8 7 6 5 4 3 2 1

PURSUIT

CHAPTER 1

Half an hour before dawn, Casey Day stumbled out of his room at the boarding-house. Out back, he stuck his head under the stream from the pump, scrubbed vigorously, then dried himself on the soiled towel that hung from a nail in the wall. He ran his fingers through his hair, crammed his hat on and then went along the alley until he came to the back gate of the way-station corral.

Eastward, the sky was graying. Yesterday's wind had blown all through the night across this thousand miles of open country, land as yet scarcely marked by the few settlers, travelers and Indians upon it. The same wind that now blew fresh and cool against Casey Day's face earlier had touched the buffalo-hide lodges of the Sioux in Dakota territory, those of Arapaho and Cheyenne here in Colorado. It would blow itself out in the high deserts where Comanches and

7

Apaches rode.

It had raced across the high country, and sighed through the pines beneath which bearded miners scratched the rocky beds of mountain streams for gold. It had stirred the shaggy hair of half-wild cattle, of antelope and of buffalo, here on the plain. Now it made a steady hum in the telegraph line that passed through town a hundred yards to the south of the stageline way station.

Casey went through the gate into the corral and climbed to the loft where the hay was stored. He picked up the pitchfork, but for a moment he did not use it, ignoring the dozen or so head of horses that gathered below and began to bite and kick for a place at the manger.

Instead, he stared out at the lightening plain, his face somber, his eyes touched with bitterness.

It rankled a man to be shelved, especially when the shelving was unjust. It rankled particularly when he was young and strong, eager to make his mark on the world. It had rankled in Casey Day for three years, and now he asked himself how much longer he'd be stuck away here in this remote place. He didn't know, but it wasn't going to be for long. He'd see to that himself.

Casey was a tall man of twenty-five. His

shoulders were broad — they came alive under his thin blue shirt with long, rippling muscles as he worked.

His face was roughhewn and craggy, with sharp angles and flat planes. His straight nose was a bit too large, his mouth wide and firm, his chin an outcropping of stubborn strength.

For a few minutes he pitched hay steadily, and when he finished it filled the manger with precise exactness, nowhere thin, nowhere spilling over. A minimum of wastage lay on the ground.

Now, the sky was growing pink to eastward, and Casey leaned against the door jamb of the loft to watch its changing beauty.

Buffalo Wallow sprawled in almost the exact center of a bowl formed by nature. At times Casey thought it resembled sediment collected here by liquid long since evaporated.

A mile southeast of the town was the buffalo wallow from which the town got its name, filled today with water left over from the heavy rain of a week before. Its surface reflected the rose-gold of the eastern cloud layer.

Three or four miles north of town stood a gray sandstone bluff; on its face the double switchback of the descending stageroad was visible. From the foot of the bluff, the road led arrow-straight into town where it became Main Street briefly before continuing south and west toward Denver City and the distant mountains.

Over the rim of the bowl to the east there suddenly appeared a file of horsemen. Casey counted four. He squinted, trying to make them out, but they were too far off for identification.

Casey shrugged, climbed down and began to pump water for the horse trough. He worked steadily and without stopping for fifteen minutes — then the trough was full. He climbed back to the loft and again studied the approaching horsemen, who were now less than a quarter-mile away.

Except for their leader, they were dressed in fringed buckskin pants and shirts, no doubt traded from the squaws in some Indian village, and one wore a hip-length leather coat. Two of them appeared to be wearing high-heeled boots of the kind used in Texas. A third wore Arapaho moccasins, Casey guessed, for he could see the lavish quill decorations upon them. The fourth, in front, wore a cavalry officer's riding boots and what looked like Army spurs.

Their hats were wide-brimmed cavalry

hats, two greenish black, one dusty gray; and the contrast drew a spare smile from Casey's mouth. Their leader wore an ancient gray beaver hat.

He was different in one other respect. Instead of buckskins he wore a soiled, disreputable gray broadcloth suit, and the wearing of it seemed to set him apart and mark him their leader.

He paused at the edge of town, swiveled around in his saddle and spoke to his three companions. Then he turned and came on again, his head swinging to right and left as though he were memorizing each detail of the town.

Casey's glance swept over it. Eighteen buildings in all, counting the ramshackle barn at the rear of the way station. They sat on both sides of Main and both sides of another unnamed street a block east of Main. All were of rough-sawed pine and all were unpainted. Casey knew that half of them were empty. And they all had a temporary appearance, as though this town were not quite sure it was going to stay. The east side of Main boasted a boardwalk. The west side had only a dusty path.

The town was waking now, stirring after its night of rest. Smoke arose from two or three chimneys.

The four men passed the schoolhouse and a dog got up, walked out to intercept them, wagging his stubby tail tentatively. The leader of the four must have spoken to him, for the dog fell in behind his horse.

The men, with the dog, crossed Main, lining up then at the hitchrail before the boardinghouse. They dismounted stiffly, and stretched, as though they had been riding all night.

Casey climbed down from the loft, went back along the alley to the rear of the boardinghouse, and now he washed again, this time running a comb through his stiff black hair.

He circled the boardinghouse. The man in the beaver hat was just now climbing the steps to the veranda, his coat bunching over the holstered Colt's Navy revolver at his waist.

His face was thin and hollow-cheeked. It was covered with a soft black beard stubble. His mouth was sensitive, his nose straight and very narrow, almost pointed.

But it was his eyes that drew and held Casey's attention; they were wells of darkness in which nothing was visible — nothing cold or warm, nothing either of human intelligence or animal shrewdness. They were like a very small infant's eyes, seeing, but empty of reaction as if nothing went on behind them.

Glancing at Casey, the man went in, followed by the dog and by his three companions. Casey followed. The man in the beaver hat looked across the big dining room at Grace Loftus in the kitchen doorway and said, "My name's Bell." He swung his head, indicating his three companions. He introduced them in the order in which they stood beside the door. "Wagner . . . Moya . . . Buck. Can you give us some breakfast?"

Casey thought Grace Loftus' voice was sharper than usual. "I can. It'll be twenty-five cents apiece. Now get that dirty mongrel out of here and wash. Breakfast in ten minutes."

Bell spoke without turning his head. "Get him out, like the lady says."

Wagner, the big one, picked up the dog by the scruff of the neck. He opened the door and dropped the dog outside.

Bell smiled with his lips, his eyes empty and without emotion. "The dog's out. Where do we wash and how do we get there?"

"Same way you came in. Walk around the side to the back." The sharpness in Grace's voice was edged with impatience. Casey thought he saw an odd little flame kindle in

Bell's eyes. But the man turned away and followed the others through the door.

Casey grinned at Grace Loftus. "Which side of the bed did you get out of this morning?"

She did not return his smile. "Wrong side, I guess." A small frown creased her smooth forehead. "Haven't you ever disliked someone the moment you saw him?"

"I guess I have."

She was thoughtful, and her frown lingered. "Maybe it's his eyes — or the lines in his face. He's cruel. It's written all over him."

"I know."

She started to turn, then swung back. "What do they want? Why are they traveling in a bunch like that?"

Casey chuckled. "Good sense to travel in a bunch — discourages the Arapaho from trying to lift your hair."

Grace returned to the kitchen. On impulse, Casey followed and went to the window. Looking out, he saw the big one, Wagner, working the pump for the others.

The pump stood in the middle of the lean-to floor. The floor around it was covered with corrugated iron, so that waste water would run off and not trickle back into the well.

Bell and the others washed vigorously, not talking. They toweled themselves dry and then headed back around the boardinghouse toward the front door.

Casey went back in and sat down. A tall, burly man, blond and handsome, came in and sat down beside Casey. "Mornin'. Who do the four horses belong to?"

"Morning, Shawcross. Some strangers. Just rode in."

Alan Shawcross was a saddle trader. He kept a bunch of oxen out on the grass near town for trading with travelers whose oxen were exhausted and sore-footed. He employed two Mexicans as herders, and stayed in town himself.

The four strangers came in and seated themselves across the long table. Casey studied them openly. Wagner, seated, looked even bigger than he did standing. His shoulders were half again as broad as average. His neck was a solid column of muscle, his chest deep and strong as a stallion's. His eyes had a calculating, greedy look to them.

The one called Moya was no more than medium height and slightly built. He wore his hair long, nearly to his shoulders; it was mouse-colored, uncombed and dirty. Casey's eyes passed on to the fourth, called Buck.

This one was older, perhaps forty-five. His hair was grizzled, his beard stubble gray. His eyes, gray as his beard, were hard and cold and direct.

From the kitchen came the smell of frying pork and boiling coffee. Grace Loftus came in with a large tray filled with fried potatoes. She handed the tray to Shawcross, who smiled up at her intimately and confidently, as though this had been a sign of her favor.

Two more men came in and sat down, both looking sick. Casey heard one of them say to the other in a low voice, "We'll both feel better after we get a little food in our bellies. Then we can ride out."

Just then he got a whiff of the frying pork and his face turned gray. He got up and hurried out, a hand over his mouth.

Casey grinned. These two were cowhands from the Ramirez ranch back west of town. Casey had seen them in Pelton's saloon last night; from the looks of them this morning, they'd stayed at Pelton's too long.

Grace returned, this time carrying a platter of fried side meat in one hand, a pot of steaming coffee in the other. She handed the platter to Shawcross and filled Casey's cup with coffee.

Casey sipped it gratefully, a big man, raw-boned and long muscled, with a lean sparseness about him. He weighed a hundred and eighty, but he could have weighed two hundred without being fat or fleshy. His eyes were blue, wide-set and sharp, and now they studied Bell almost covertly, for an elusive memory was stirring in the back of his mind.

Bell looked up and met his glance, but still Casey's memory of the man stubbornly remained hazy.

The platters passed from hand to hand, and Grace Loftus moved around, filling and refilling coffee cups. All of the men ate noisily and quickly. Shawcross pulled out a cigar, and Casey began to pack his pipe. Grace returned to the kitchen.

Bell shoved his chair back and stood up, swiftly drawing the gun at his waist. Its hammer click was somehow soft and deadly. He spoke to Moya, the slight one. "Get that woman back in here."

Moya chuckled almost soundlessly and headed for the kitchen, his moccasins making a small hissing sound upon the floor. After a moment, Casey heard her gasp, her muffled, angry words. After that he heard the resounding smack of her hand striking Moya's cheek. A small grin played at the corners of Casey's mouth.

But the grin faded as, from the kitchen,

there came a frightened scream, then the sound of a body slamming against a wall.

Casey started to his feet, but before he could gain them, Wagner leaned over the table and clamped his monstrous hand on Casey's right wrist. Bell said, "That's right, hold him. I don't want to kill him."

Casey tried to tear free, but it was like trying to pull his wrist from a vise. Before he quite realized what was happening, Wagner had vaulted the table, scattering dishes to the floor and, with a deft twist, brought Casey's right arm around behind his back, whirling him as he did. His voice was deep, surprisingly calm. "Be still, you, or I'll break your arm." He raised Casey's arm toward his shoulder blades and twisted enough to make it crack. Sweat popped out on Casey's forehead.

Something about the man's incredible strength, the calm tone of his voice, convinced Casey he would do exactly that. So Casey stopped struggling. Then there came a whimpering sound from the kitchen, and it brought raw fury to Casey's eyes. He began to struggle again. Wagner's grip tightened, and the arm cracked again. Dizziness washed in waves through Casey's head.

Shawcross half rose in his chair, blustering. "Now see here, whoever you are, you can't . . ."

Bell put his empty eyes on the man. "You goin' to stop us?"

Shawcross looked at Buck, back at Bell, and then at Casey, whose face was contorted in agony. He lost color and sank back into his chair. He didn't speak again.

The hungover cowboy seemed dazed, as though he couldn't quite believe what was happening. He was obviously very sick.

Bell said, "Check 'em for guns, Buck."

Buck moved around the table. He got a revolver from a holster at Casey's side, and one from the cowhand who surrendered it without protest. He found a holdout gun on Shawcross, a pepperbox. He stuffed the two revolvers into his belt and dropped the derringer into the pocket of his leather coat.

The whimpering continued in the kitchen. Bell's voice turned sharp. "Bring her in! I said we were going to push these people just as far as we had to and no farther."

Grace Loftus came through the door, propelled by Moya, who held her in a grip similar to the one Wagner had on Casey, right arm high against her shoulder blades. The bodice of her dress was torn, and she clutched it together with her free left hand.

Bell said, "Let her go!"

19

Moya released her. His face was flushed and he was smiling oddly; his breathing was shallow and quick. Bell said, looking at the girl, "Sit down and be quiet."

Grace Loftus' sharpness was all gone. Moya had left her with only terror. She sank into a chair and sat there, shuddering, looking from Moya to Bell and back at Moya again.

Bell spoke to the group. "We'll be in town until midmorning. If everyone does exactly as they're told, nobody'll get hurt. If they don't . . ."

The cowhand's face had been getting paler, grayer by the minute. Suddenly he jumped to his feet and lunged for the door.

He got about halfway. Bell's gun roared once. Smoke billowed from its muzzle, acrid and blinding.

The cowboy stumbled, went to his knees. He stayed that way for an instant, and looked around, surprise etched on his face. Surprise and shock and puzzlement. He started to retch, but the life in him was ebbing fast and he folded to the floor and lay still. A red stain began to spread slowly over the back of his shirt.

Bell's voice was thin and high. "Damn it, now do as you're told, or you'll all get that."

CHAPTER 2

Bell, with the still smoking gun in his hand, held their fascinated stares for a moment. Casey pulled against Wagner's cruel grip on his twisted arm. "For God's sake, he was sick, that's all! He wasn't going to try anything!"

Bell nodded at Wagner, and the big man put a little extra pressure on Casey's arm. "Shut up, you," Bell said.

Casey's mouth was twisted with pain. "The hell I will! What's this all about, anyhow?"

Bell looked imperturbably at Casey. "We want that special stagecoach, mister. You run the way station and you know how it'll be guarded. There'll be a driver and a shotgun guard on the box. Two men with rifles inside. Two outriders in front, two behind. We'd never get near it on the road, but here in town it'll be different. They feel safe when they pull into town; they're always off guard for a few minutes. I know; I've watched them. The driver and the guard'll be climbing down off the box. The guards inside'll be getting out. The outriders'll be heading for the corral to change horses." He paused and grinned at Casey, obviously pleased with himself.

"That's when we'll hit them."

He turned his head and looked at Moya. "Look around outside and see if anybody heard the shot. Then bring that other cowhand in."

Moya left. Casey stared at Bell with incredulous anger. "You'll never get away with it."

"We know there's going to be a hundred and fifty thousand in currency on that special coach consigned to a bank in Denver City. We want it. We're going to have it if we have to kill everybody in this Goddamn town. Everybody, understand? Men, women, *and* kids."

Casey's mouth worked with his effort to control his anger. "You think you can get away afterward?"

Bell's smile didn't waver. "I know we can. First, your corral is going to be filled with dead horses. Second, we're going to take a quarter-mile section of the telegraph wire with us. By the time the news gets out we'll be a couple hundred miles away."

The room was silent as its shocked occupants considered what Bell had said. Moya came in, prodding the pale-faced cowpuncher along with the puncher's own gun. Bell said, "Drag the other one outside."

Moya took the dead man's feet and hauled

him out through the kitchen. The dead man's head thumped against the board floor of the lean-to as Moya dragged him through the door.

The remaining puncher stared at Bell. "Why'd you do it?"

"He didn't do what he was told. Now shut up, or I'll give you the same." Bell's voice was level and hard.

The puncher began to shake as though he was cold. He didn't speak again.

Bell said, "Wagner, you and Moya stay here and watch this bunch. Buck and me are going out and bring the others in."

He waited until Moya had returned. Then he went out the door, Buck following close on his heels.

Casey Day had never been as ragingly furious as he was now. But in the grip of the giant, Wagner, he was helpless. He knew that if he struggled Wagner would make good his threat, and a broken right arm would hardly be an asset in the approaching crisis.

He glanced across at Grace Loftus. She was watching Moya with a mesmerized fascination. Casey had never seen her like this before. Ordinarily she was self-possessed and self-sufficient. But her encounter with Moya had stolen these qualities from her and she was solidly in the grip of fear.

There was suddenly something very familiar in this for Casey. Grace's terror — his own helplessness.

He remembered another time, another place. Denver City, raw and new and filled with gold seekers until it overflowed . . .

Casey had had a good job with the stage company there, and was heading for a better one. He was one of their best men, they said.

There was a gold shipment under Casey's care in the company's office safe. Only Casey knew the combination. There was a girl in the office, too — a terrified girl who didn't want to die. Casey didn't value gold against a human life. He opened the safe and the girl lived. Casey lived too, although the blow on his head didn't come far from killing him.

It hadn't been easy to explain the loss of the gold. The stageline was new, hard-pressed for capital. The girl's life wasn't relatively as important to its owners as it had been to Casey. There were suspicions voiced that Casey had made things too easy for the outlaws, suspicions that he had shared in the gold itself. There was nothing provable, of course. But they sent Casey out here to Buffalo Wallow to rot. He'd been here more than three years, growing more bitter every year. . . .

Moya's voice pulled him back to the present. It was soft, almost eager. "Let him go, Wagner. Let him go. Let's see what he does."

"But Bell said . . ."

"He said watch 'em, not hold 'em." Moya's voice was thin; his breathing had grown shallow again.

Casey felt his arm drop. He brought it around in front of him and began to rub its twisted muscles. All the time his anger was mounting. He could feel it rising in the form of an unthinking recklessness. He could feel it in the tension of his arms and legs, a tension that only action could ease.

Moya watched him, bright-eyed, for a few moments. Moya's gun was loosely held in his right hand, and there was an expectant readiness in the man.

Casey longed to smash his fist into Moya's face. His hands clenched until the knuckles were white. But he held himself still, remembering the puncher who had started to go outside.

Moya was slim and wiry, his body giving an impression of considerable physical strength. His skin was tanned dark, but he somehow appeared sallow. A thin, straggling black beard stubble shadowed his jaw and his hollow cheeks. His slack lips were often parted in a mirthless smile, revealing teeth that were yellowed and, in places, black. His eyes were pale brown — Casey thought of them as dun — but within them were little dancing flecks of a lighter color.

Moya said tauntingly, "If they're all as yellow as this one, we will not have trouble this morning."

Casey's tensing body must have been apparent to everyone. Shawcross said quickly, urgently, "Casey! Don't do it! Can't you see that's just what he wants?"

But Casey had already snatched up a chair and flung it across the table at Moya. Moya ducked and the chair smashed against the wall. Casey followed the chair, vaulting across the table with what seemed a single movement. Grace Loftus screamed. Moya put a bullet into the floor at Casey's feet, then raised the muzzle until it centered steadily on Casey's belly.

Casey stopped, as though he had run into a wall. Moya's eyes told him that if he advanced another step he'd get the same treatment the sick cowpuncher had got.

Moya was chuckling softly. He said to Wagner, "Bell told us to push 'em as far as we had to. This one needs some pushing. Get hold of his arms."

Casey whirled to face the giant, who shoved aside the long table as though it were a toy. Anger still smoldered in Casey, but there was bitterness and defeat in him now as well. A gun at his back, a man twice his size before him.

He started a swing at Wagner, timing it so that the man's own forward momentum would add to its force. But Moya moved in behind him like a cat and struck the side of his head with the revolver barrel.

Casey went to his knees, the room whirling before his eyes. Wagner moved around behind him and yanked him up, using the same vicious armlock he had used before. Casey felt his shoulder muscles tear loose; excruciating pain flooded through him. He struggled, but Wagner's grip only tightened. Sweat broke out all over Casey's body.

As though from a distance he heard Moya's voice. "All of you watch this. It might make the rest of the morning easier for everybody."

Casey knew he didn't mean it. This was not going to be an example to the others. This was something Moya was going to enjoy. Suddenly Moya poked his revolver barrel savagely into Casey's middle.

Pain shot from the area like an explosion. Casey doubled forward involuntarily against the holding pressure of Wagner's arms. He brought his foot down savagely upon Wagner's instep. The big man grunted with pain, and raised Casey's twisted arm viciously.

Only the powerful muscles of Casey's arm and shoulder prevented the arm from breaking. As it was, he was lifted from the floor, and hung there a moment until Wagner let him down again.

Before the pain in his arm and his belly had begun to subside, Moya's revolver barrel came slashing across Casey's jaw, turned so that the front side raked the flesh. A two-inch gash opened along his jawline. It began to bleed freely, the blood running down his neck and soaking his collar. Again the revolver barrel slashed, and this time it opened a horizontal cut half the width of Casey's forehead. This one, too, began to bleed, and the blood ran down into Casey's eyes.

Grace Loftus whimpered, "Please! For God's sake, stop it! Please!"

Moya chuckled. And again the revolver barrel stabbed into Casey's middle. Casey fought nausea desperately and lost. He doubled over and gagged.

Moya's voice was high and strange. "Is

this the toughest one in town?" Casey could no longer see him; there was too much blood in his eyes.

Moya said, "The gun's too easy. Let's make it last a while."

The first blow flattened Casey's lips against his teeth. The second closed his right eye. Half insensible, he waited for a third which never landed. He heard Bell's sharp voice from the direction of the door. "Moya! Damn you, that's enough! Wagner, let him go."

Casey was freed. Reeling, he fumbled for his bandanna and mopped his battered face. He didn't care if they killed him. All he wanted to do was to get his hands on Moya. He cleared the blood from his eyes and blinked. He got his legs steady under him and with an animal growl sounding deep in his throat, he threw himself at Moya.

There was satisfaction in the solid way his body struck the other. He felt Moya go back, and fell with him, groping for the hand that held the gun. He got it, and clung with all his strength.

Moya twisted, raising his knees to protect his belly. Casey, lying across him, brought an elbow down across his throat and heard him choke. He raised the elbow, moved it aside, then brought it smashing back into

Moya's face.

Moya tried to roll, but Casey leaped astride him and began to hammer Moya's face with his free right hand.

He felt himself lifted clear by a hand that grasped his shirt from behind. The shirt tore and he fell back. Wagner caught him again, lifted him, whirled him around and backhanded him on the side of the head.

Casey's head rang. Bright lights flashed before his eyes. Wagner pushed him into a chair. "Quit, you damned fool! You want to get yourself killed?"

Moya was up now, and coming for him, but Bell's voice, sharp as the lash of a whip, stopped him. Moya's eyes looked pure murder at Casey and Casey glared back. Blood ran from Moya's nose, and he wiped at it with a grimy buckskin sleeve.

Bell was breathing fast, as though he had been running. "Moya, you come with me. Damn it, can't I trust you out of my sight?"

Moya started to say something, but Bell cut him short as he spoke to the other two. "Buck, you and Wagner stay this time."

The blur that had obscured Casey's vision began to clear. He saw Bell and Moya go out the door and caught Moya's quick-flung backward glance. The look was a promise, and in spite of himself Casey felt a chill. He thought, "He's crazy. He's as crazy as hell!"

The chair felt good under him. He dropped his head low between his knees and waited for the nausea and dizziness to pass. Blood dripped from his face to the floor.

The others in the room were silent, as though a single word from any of them would bring on the same treatment Casey had received — or a bullet like the one that had cut down the cowpuncher. Casey raised his head and looked at Buck.

Buck was a grizzled-looking man. He had a solid body thickness that looked slow and heavy. His way of walking, however, belied the impression. He moved quickly, surely, without waste motion.

His face was covered with several days' growth of graying whiskers. His nose, flattened and crooked, gave him the tough look of a prize fighter. Bushy tufts of hair protruded from his nostrils and the pores on his nose were plainly visible. His eyes were gray, calm, steady eyes that never reflected any warmth. He was like some wild animal, impersonal, calm enough unless threatened, but savage and dangerous.

His gun was carried low on a sagging belt, and tied with a thong of rawhide to his thigh. Besides this gun, he had Casey's and the dead cowhand's thrust into his belt and

Shawcross' pepperbox in the side pocket of his leather coat.

Buck said suddenly to Wagner, "Take him out and let him wash at the pump. Take him back through the kitchen. We don't want to stir up the rest of the town just yet."

Wagner said tonelessly, "Come on, you."

Casey lifted himself from the chair with an effort. His body ached and his head reeled. For a moment he thought he would fall. Straightening slowly, he followed Wagner into the kitchen and out the back door. None of the others in the room even looked at him. Outside, he saw the dead puncher's body, laying face up in the sun where Moya had left it.

A feeling of unreality assailed Casey. This was like a nightmare. But this was no dream and there'd be no waking, no relief. It would go on until the stage came in.

Somehow Casey had to stop them. Somehow. Old man Grinstead, the stageline owner, would have a stroke if Bell and his men got away with this. This would be more than a mere gold shipment holdup. This would be life or death for the stageline. If the outlaws got away with it, the line would be finished. Grinstead too, and a lifetime of building. Likewise Casey, for the story would follow him wherever he went. He'd be the man who had let outlaws ruin the Grinstead line. No transportation company in the west would give him a job after that.

Casey Day had always been able to handle anything that came along. Until that damned holdup in Denver City. And now this . . .

A chill coursed his spine. He knew a sudden fear that he might die today. Sometime during the morning death would come, from Moya, from Bell, from the one called Buck or from Wagner. It would come, and not only to him, but to others in the town. And Casey couldn't stop it. Unless he could get the town to unite somehow.

His mouth twisted suddenly. Like they'd united back there in the boardinghouse dining room? He could still see Shawcross, big and burly and strong, but not even getting out of his chair. He could still hear Shawcross' feeble protest over the way Moya was manhandling Grace Loftus in the kitchen.

The sun, blazing into the lean-to behind the boardinghouse, dazzled and blinded him. When he squinted against it, pain shot from the ragged tear on his forehead and fresh blood ran into his brows. He felt sick and dizzy.

Wagner worked the pump handle. Casey

stuck his head under the icy stream that gushed from its spout. He let it run over his head for a few moments and its coldness shocked him back to full consciousness. His head began to ache with persistent intensity.

He slopped water onto his face with his cupped hands. Wagner reached over and got the filthy towel. He held it in the water until it was soaked and then handed it to Casey. "Hold that against them cuts. Maybe it'll stop the bleedin'." He might have been telling someone how to treat an injured horse.

Casey did as he was told, and after a while the bleeding slowed down. He rinsed out the towel and wrung it dry. Then he went back into the boardinghouse dining room, mopping his face with it. He looked at Buck. "You going to hold us here until the stage gets in?" He was hoping Buck would say yes, for the complete absence of people on the streets would put the stagecoach crew on guard.

Buck shook his head. "We'll hold some of you as hostages, so's the others'll behave. The rest of you can go about your business, as soon as Bell says so, anyway. You'll be down at the way station like always. We aim to have things look real normal."

"You think my face looks normal?"

Buck grinned crookedly. "Judgin' from

that temper of yours, I'd say it did."

Grace Loftus seemed to have gathered courage from Moya's absence. She spoke now to Buck in a voice both timid and angry. "Casey needs attention."

"Give it to him, then."

She got up and went to the kitchen. Wagner went along, towering over her like a giant.

After a few moments she came back with a jar of salve and a box of court plaster. She salved the cuts on Casey's face, then covered them with strips of court plaster. Her face was pale and her eyes were sick. She bent close, as though to study her work. Her voice was a frightened whisper. "Casey, stop fighting them. If we do what they say, maybe no one else will get hurt. You can't beat them all alone. So why try?"

Casey looked at her, his eyes surprised. She was saying it was foolish to fight unless you knew you could win. It was an attitude foreign to Casey's nature.

She whispered urgently, "Casey, let them alone and they'll let us alone."

"You don't really believe that, do you?"

"Yes, I do!" Her words were desperate, too emphatic.

Buck broke in harshly. "Shut up, you two."

Casey looked at him. He said deliberately,

35

"Yes, sir."

Buck met Casey's defiant glance with his own. A new, colder light began to burn in Buck's eyes, a light that meant he didn't like Casey. He said, "You can't learn, can you? All right. Keep it up. You'll be layin' alongside our friend out back before you're through."

Casey felt the wildness stir in him. Then Grace's hand was on his shoulder. He looked up at her and she shook her head almost imperceptibly.

He thought bitterly that she wanted him to be like Shawcross and the others. Sit still in a chair while they manhandled a girl. Take all the damned insults they wanted to hand out. Be a worm for the sake of staying alive.

He looked around the room. Grace had seated herself in a chair next to him. She wasn't looking at him. She wasn't looking at anything. She was probably telling herself that this wasn't real. It was a dream, and if she sat real still, it would fade and go away. Her hands, clasped in her lap, were trembling.

He remembered something she had once told him. "Casey, in that holdup over in Denver you did what any sensible man would do. You put human life against money, and the human life won. I admire you for it. And I hate your old stage company for expecting more. Give it up, Casey. Don't give this country your life for nothing."

He had said, "What do you want me to do, Grace?"

"Go back East," she had answered. "Take me with you. Back there things are more civilized. No one will expect more of you than you can give."

He knew that Grace had never been contented here. She had stayed only because the boardinghouse was all her father had left her and she had been unable to sell it. Having to stay here had made her sharp and sour just as being shoved out here to rot had embittered Casey. Perhaps it was this bitterness that had drawn them together.

Casey's head still throbbed. He ignored the pain, trying to force his mind to find some way out of this thing that threatened the town, out of the trouble Casey himself was in. If Bell's gang succeeded in pulling this job off, Casey was finished. He always wound up with that.

He thought of the other men in the town, the ones Bell and Moya had gone out to fetch. Not much hope there.

Little Darrel Gooch, the telegraph operator, didn't even have the courage to defy his own buxom, domineering wife. Casey scarcely counted on him to stand up to four armed and vicious outlaws.

Then there was Matt Housman. Matt wouldn't fight back, either. He knew his wife, Marian, was fooling around with Alan Shawcross, but he lacked the guts to stop it.

No, neither Gooch nor Housman would be of any help. Casey looked across at Shawcross, and wondered wryly what Marian Housman would have thought of him today. Not much, he guessed. Shawcross hadn't exactly been a tiger. . . .

Well, there was Pelton, who ran the saloon. He was all right. He'd probably put up a hell of a fight if he got the chance. Casey doubted if he'd get the chance.

Then there was Etheridge. A big man, Etheridge, fully as big as Shawcross, though most of his bulk was fat. But Etheridge was the town's lay preacher and had religious scruples against violence.

Gooch, Housman, Etheridge and Pelton . . . Pelton was the only one who would fight. Casey tasted the bitterness of frustration. The pain in his head and in the torn, twisted ligaments and muscles of his right arm suddenly engulfed him.

He slumped down in his chair. The room

was silent, save for Buck's impatient, continuously tapping finger against the table top. Again Casey felt that death was very close.

Yet why hadn't they killed him a while ago? Bell hadn't hesitated an instant about killing the cowpuncher. Why had he hesitated about killing Casey?

They needed him! They needed him to show himself when the stage came in. Otherwise the guards might become suspicious.

The realization gave a boost to his spirits. If they needed him, if they didn't want him dead, then he had a chance. A slim one, but a chance . . .

CHAPTER 3

They sat, and the time ran on silently except for the slight sound of their breathing.

After what Casey judged to be half an hour, he heard steps upon the boardinghouse veranda. The door opened and Amanda Gooch came in, followed by her husband and by Bell and Moya.

She was a big, gray-haired woman whose face managed to be both flabby and hard. Her eyes, usually a cold blue, were now filled with uncertainty and fear. There was a flaming red mark on one side of her face and blood trickled from a corner of her mouth.

She glanced once at Casey's face, then looked quickly, almost fearfully away. Her eyes went to her husband accusingly, and somehow this angered Casey. What the hell did she expect from him? She'd spent the fifteen years of her marriage trying to break him, and she'd succeeded. Did she think he'd turn into a hero now?

She settled into a chair that creaked loudly beneath her weight. Bell said, "Come on, Gooch. Let's go over to your office. It'd give things away if you wasn't at that telegraph key. But don't forget that I know the code. And remember what'll happen to your wife if you make a mistake."

Darrel Gooch was a small man. His hair was gone from the crown of his head and thinning over his forehead. His shoulders had a permanent stoop, maybe from discouragement, maybe from bending over his telegraph key. Casey didn't know.

Gooch looked at his wife as he turned. His eyes held an expression of pity mixed with triumph. Casey could see that for once the little man held the upper hand and knew it. Upon his actions at the telegraph office depended his wife's safety, perhaps her very life.

He went out and Bell followed.

They were gone for about ten minutes, and then Bell came back. He was sucking the knuckles of his right hand. Casey could see they were skinned and bleeding, and he knew wonder . . . Somewhere Gooch must have found the courage to resist. And Bell had worked him over with his fists.

Bell said to Casey, "All right. Who else lives in this town?"

"I thought you knew all the answers."

"Maybe. But I figure you can bring me up to date. It's been two months since I was here."

Casey was silent, remembering Bell at last. The man had come through Buffalo Wallow by stage a couple of months ago, and had stayed in town overnight because the Cheyennes were cutting up between here and Denver. Bell had asked a lot of questions, Casey recalled.

Bell's mouth tightened. "Talk, man, or I'll turn Moya loose on you again."

Casey, checking an angry retort, threw a murderous glance at Moya. Moya's eyes burned back at him.

Bell repeated, "Talk! I haven't got all day."

Casey said, "Go to hell."

Bell's voice was soft and quick. "All right, Wagner."

Casey knew he couldn't stand another round with Moya. Not now. He couldn't and be ready when the chance came — if it came. He said, "Never mind. I'll tell you. There's Nick Pelton. He runs the saloon. He's got three kids that are half Arapaho, but his wife's dead. The kids are the reason the Arapaho and Cheyenne leave the town alone, I guess." He was stringing out, wasting time for Bell.

"All right. All right. Who else?"

"Housman. Matt Housman, that is. He's got a wife and a fifteen-year-old boy. His wife's name is Marian."

"Yeah? What's that storekeeper's name?"

"Etheridge."

"What about him?"

Casey said wearily, "He's our part-time preacher. He's got a wife and three daughters, Faith, Hope and Charity. He's also got a son, Pete. Pete's riding shotgun guard on the stage you're after."

"Anyone else?"

"No."

"You're a lair, Day. There's another woman in town, I remember. That dressmaker. What's her name?"

"Lorene Mowrey." Uneasiness stirred in

Casey. He couldn't help glancing at Moya. He thought about Lorene Mowrey a moment, picturing her in his mind. . . .

Bell said, "All right. That all checks out. Come on, Moya. We'll go get Housman next."

He started toward the door, followed by Moya, but at that moment Lorene Mowrey came in from outside. She looked at the group in startled surprise before her glance settled on Casey. Compassion leaped into her eyes. "Casey! What happened to you?"

Ignoring the others she crossed the room to him. He stood up to face her. One of her hands reached up, as though she would touch his lacerated jaw. Casey moved his head aside self-consciously. He said quickly, "Lorene, it's nothing."

Bell interrupted with sly, hopeful malice. "This your sweetie, Day?"

Color flamed in Lorene Mowrey's face. Her eyes blazed as she turned and looked at Bell. Casey caught her by the shoulders. "Sit down, Lorene, and be quiet."

He pushed her gently into a chair. Turning, he saw that Moya was looking at her. He held onto his flaring temper with difficulty.

Lorene Mowrey was a small girl, coming just to the point of Casey's shoulder. Her hair, honey-colored, was done in a mass of curls pinned behind her head. Her skin was pale as the petals of a sand lily. Her large, wide-set eyes were sometimes green, sometimes gray. Her mouth was full, the lips expressive, usually quick to smile, a warm-natured, provocative mouth.

But to Casey, the most noticeable thing about Lorene Mowrey was her serenity. Nothing ever disturbed or broke it; even now it was intact in spite of the potential violence of the situation.

Casey, looked from her to Grace Loftus and back again. It struck him that he'd never compared the two before. Suddenly he knew that Lorene Mowrey would never be irritable or cross. Nor would she ever become as pathetically terrified as Grace Loftus was now . . .

Bell said, "Tell her, Day."

Casey said gently, "They want the coach that comes in at ten, Lorene. It's supposed to have a hundred and fifty thousand in currency on it. It's too strong to jump on the road, so they're going to jump it here in town while the men with it are off guard. Meanwhile, they're taking over the town to see that nobody interferes." He looked at Moya. "They're trigger crazy and mean, so

44

do what they say. They've already killed one man."

"Who?" Her voice was a whisper.

"One of Ramirez' punchers, in town for a bust."

Bell pulled an enormous silver watch from his pocket, opened its cover and looked at it. He said, "All right. We'll hold onto the Loftus girl and Lorene and the old woman. We'll keep the puncher, too; he's got nothing to do but get over his big head. We'll get Housman's wife and somebody from the Etheridge family and after that you can all go on about your business. Only remember that cowboy lyin' out back. Don't do anything that'll make you join him."

Nobody answered. Casey glanced around at the ring of frightened faces. His eye caught and held on Amanda Gooch's face.

Panic was growing in her eyes. Casey sensed she was going to run before she moved. None of the outlaws happened to be watching her. Bell had his glance on Casey. Moya was looking at Lorene. Wagner and Buck were watching Bell.

For a heavy woman, Amanda Gooch could move surprisingly fast. She heaved herself to her feet, whirled and lumbered toward the door, hampered by her long skirts as well as by her own huge bulk. But terror lent her speed.

Bell leaped in pursuit. Moya followed. Buck's and Wagner's glances swiveled to follow the fleeing woman, though they didn't move.

Casey's muscles tensed. But he knew he had no chance against the four. He also knew he shouldn't throw away what chance he did have for the sake of a panic-stricken woman.

Yet he knew that if one of the four should draw a gun and point it at the fleeing woman, he'd have to try to reach the one who held it. But none of them drew a gun.

Bell caught her as she went through the door. There was a brief scuffle on the porch, then Moya and Bell dragged her back inside.

Her face was a ghastly, pasty gray. Her eyes were dilated with fear. Her mouth worked ludicrously and a muscle twitched in one flabby cheek. They gave her a hard push and she staggered across the room and fell to the floor. The building shook under the impact of her heavy body.

Anger showed in Bell's eyes for the first time. His face was flushed. "Damn it," he shouted. "Are you all stupid? What do I have to do to show you I mean business?"

Lorene Mowrey looked at him coldly, then got up from her chair and went to Amanda

Gooch. She knelt on the floor beside her, calming her in a soft voice whose words were not distinguishable to Casey.

The others sat or stood, motionless, as though frozen by fear and afraid to move.

Mark Housman, probably having seen the scuffle on his way to school, chose this moment to come bursting in.

Buck's hand dropped to the grip of his gun. Wagner hunched his shoulders a little and started forward. Moya stood watchful and tense behind the boy. Bell swung around quickly to face Mark.

There was too much tension in the four, too much nervous readiness. They were all jumpy now, Casey thought, too jumpy to be relied upon to act sanely.

He said quickly, "Easy, son. Everything's all right."

The boy looked at the woman on the floor, then at Casey's battered and bandaged face. His eyes were wide and scared. "What do you mean, all right? Things — well, what's going on?"

Casey repeated patiently to Mark the story he'd told Lorene. Mark stared at him for a moment, then said shrilly, "Why don't you do something? Those men on the stage — they won't know what hit 'em!" Casey knew he was thinking of Pete Etheridge, who was the boy's idol.

Casey stared at Mark, watching impatience and rebellion rise in the boy. Mark was fifteen, almost a man in body, but still a boy in his mind. He'd never come up against anything quite like this before and he didn't know how to assess it.

He was a tall, rather thin boy, whose brown face habitually held an almost sullen expression. Now he looked across at Shawcross, his eyes hating and contemptuous. "Why don't *you* do something?"

Moya cackled, and Bell grinned. Shawcross looked up, flushing, then looked hurriedly back at the floor.

Casey said patiently, "Mark, there are four of them, they all have guns and we don't. I know how you feel. But a man can't buck odds like that."

Some of the wildness began to fade slowly from the boy's eyes, to be replaced by disillusionment.

Bell said to Moya, "Keep the kid here." He looked at Casey. "You come with me."

Casey asked, "Why me?" He didn't want to go. He didn't like the idea of leaving Lorene, or Grace either, with Moya.

"Maybe I want to show Housman and Etheridge what putting up a scrap will get them. Your face ought to be a good convincer." Bell's eyes were blank of expression but a sardonic smile played briefly on his lips. "So come on, and no arguments, mister."

Casey shrugged and gave in. It was barely possible that the walk would turn up an opportunity. Divide and conquer. A man had a better chance against two than against four.

He made himself smile at Lorene as he went past her, still kneeling beside Amanda Gooch. He glanced at Moya, and then at Buck.

His eyes returned to Moya, and Moya deliberately grinned, exposing his yellowed, uneven teeth. Then he looked appraisingly at Lorene where she knelt on the floor.

Casey's fists clenched involuntarily, but he went out the door with Bell. He was suddenly confused, wondering why he was more disturbed for Lorene's sake than for Grace's. Maybe he felt Grace was better able to take care of herself. Or maybe it was something else . . .

Outside, he looked at Bell. "There's a fine line between pushing people far enough and pushing them too far. You better not crowd too hard."

Bell stared at him, the residue of his unstable anger of a few moments before remaining in his face. "You think you have been pushed too hard?"

"Close to it. Keep a checkrein on Moya or you might find out." Casey watched Bell closely. He knew he was taking a chance warning Bell this way.

Bell said, "Maybe you ain't been pushed far enough. Maybe you're like an outlaw bronc — maybe you need to be broke good."

Wagner was moving in, as though in response to an unspoken command from Bell. Bell's face was tight, almost eager.

Casey looked at his feet. It wasn't easy. He said sourly, "All right. I've been pushed far enough." He looked up but he didn't look at Bell, afraid of what the man might see in his eyes. "Only don't try the spurs just yet. I might forget I'm broke."

He saw John Etheridge walking down the street toward them and knew it was almost eight o'clock. Bell followed his glance and then said irritably, "All right! All right! Let it go for now. I want to catch Etheridge before he gets to his store."

CHAPTER 4

Half a block behind Etheridge, Casey could see the storekeeper's three daughters crossing the open prairie between their back door and the schoolhouse. Their feet had worn a path through the high grass and they followed it now.

Faith was in the lead, a pretty girl of sixteen, whose hair was still in braids. Hope, the leggy eleven-year-old, followed, and Charity, the youngest, came last.

Downstreet, Pelton stood in the doorway of his saloon, wiping his hands on a soiled white apron and watching his own three dark-skinned children walk silently toward the schoolhouse. Pelton always had to watch those kids all the way to the schoolhouse door. If he didn't, they'd cut and run for the buffalo wallow and spend the day there playing Indian games with the small bows and arrows they had hidden in the cattails around the wallow's edge.

In this instant, here in the street, Casey realized it was three against two, and considered briefly the possibility of tackling Bell and Wagner. If only Etheridge and Pelton had some knowledge of what was up, he might have tried it. But not knowing, the pair of them would be too slow to act.

Besides, to try anything now would be to endanger the children. Casey dismissed the idea reluctantly. He looked at Etheridge again, now no more than thirty feet away.

Etheridge was a tall, gaunt man with thick bushy eyebrows above eyes that were blue and cold, without the compassion you expected in a minister's eyes. He wore a full beard that Casey had always suspected was there to conceal a chin weak and without firmness.

Etheridge eyed the damage on Casey's face, the blood on his shirt front, and his face tightened visibly with disapproval. Casey couldn't help grinning crookedly; when he did, his mouth hurt.

Bell said irritably, "All right, come on. We'll make this short."

Etheridge came to an uncertain halt in midstreet, facing the three men. Casey could see a sudden uneasiness come into his puzzled eyes.

The storekeeper opened his mouth to ask a question, but Bell cut him short. "I'll do the talking. Call your oldest girl over here."

"What for? What is this?"

Bell rammed a gun barrel into Etheridge's middle. "Don't make it harder for yourself than it already is. Call her over."

Etheridge's eyes took on an odd, trapped look. Casey couldn't tell much about his expression otherwise, because of his beard. That fire and brimstone look certainly wasn't there, Casey noticed.

Etheridge started to bluster, but his heart wasn't in it. Casey said quietly, "There's four of them, Mr. Etheridge. Two are over at the boardinghouse. They've already killed one man. Better do what they ask."

He'd never liked Etheridge, and hadn't attended church. Etheridge's fighting, he knew, would have been confined to the standard battling against sin that all these frontier ministers did; he would be ill-equipped for down-to-earth physical conflict.

Perversely, Casey's words of caution seemed to stiffen Etheridge's spine. He told Bell stubbornly, "They've got to go to school, all three of them. Besides, what do you want with Faith?"

He grunted and doubled forward as Bell's gun muzzle jabbed savagely into his middle. Making gagging, gasping sounds, he tried to draw air into his lungs. Bell said again, implacably, "Call her over here."

After a moment, Etheridge straightened. He called weakly, "Faith."

The girl began to run toward him. Casey glanced downstreet and saw Pelton disappear into the saloon. A moment later the saloon man came out, carrying the double-barreled shotgun he kept hanging on a pair of antelope horns behind his bar.

Pelton began to walk toward the group in the middle of the street. Faith must have seen Pelton coming, for she halted uncertainly. Neither Bell nor Wagner seemed to have noticed Pelton, though both of them had glanced downstreet while he was inside the saloon.

This was the time to do something. Casey had to act or Pelton was going to die. They'd see him before he got in shotgun range, cut down on him with their revolvers before he had a chance to fire.

Bell said, "What the hell's she stoppin' for? Call her again."

Again Etheridge called, "Faith, come here," but his voice broke with the fear that was rising in him.

Casey had to act before Faith came any closer. He lunged at Bell and knocked him aside. Bell's revolver roared, the bullet plowing a furrow in the street. Pelton began to run toward them carrying the shotgun at ready across his chest.

Casey grappled for Bell's revolver, trying to swing the man's body around so it would be a shield between Wagner and himself. If he could only keep them occupied until Pelton got within range . . .

Bell's revolver went off again, so close to Casey's ear that the concussion temporarily deafened him. Desperately gripping Bell's wrists, he succeeded in getting Bell between Wagner and himself, then brought up his knee viciously into Bell's groin.

Bell shouted with pain, and most of the strength went out of his arms. But he still had the gun, and his thumb still had the strength to pull back the hammer. He struggled to free himself. Casey let go Bell's left hand and went after the gun in his right with both of his own. He caught a glimpse of Etheridge, who was standing frozen, not moving. The storekeeper might have had a chance to do something a few moments ago, but now Wagner had him covered.

Etheridge didn't even have enough presence of mind to keep his eyes on Wagner. He kept glancing beyond, at Pelton advancing behind Wagner.

Casey started to yell, but it was too late. Wagner whirled abruptly.

Casey made a last, violent effort to get Bell's gun. He freed it from Bell's grip so suddenly and unexpectedly that the force of his lunge flung it aside even as he bore Bell backward and down into the dust of the street. He fell atop the outlaw, struggling to crawl beyond, to get his hands on the fallen gun.

He heard Wagner's gun, close above him,

then from farther away the boom of Pelton's shotgun. Rapid fire from the boardinghouse veranda followed.

His hand closed at last on the gun and, rolling, he tried to bring it to bear on Wagner, but a bullet from the boardinghouse exploded in the street before his face. Dust flew into his eyes. His eyelids closed over it in helpless reflex.

He was beaten, and knew it — blind, for the moment at least, and completely helpless. His eyes burned behind their closed lids; he could not force them open.

Wagner's gun was silent, and so was Pelton's. But the gun on the boardinghouse veranda sounded again and again. The bullets thudded into the street close beside Casey's head.

He flung Bell's gun away, and still flat in the street, rested on his elbows and raised his hands, palms spread out.

Nearby, Bell cursed steadily and obscenely. Bell's voice came closer until it was right over him.

Suddenly the toe of a boot sank viciously into Casey's side. He doubled and dug at his eyes with his knuckles. The boot landed again and again. Bell's voice was savage. "Damn you! I ought to kill you right where you lie!"

Casey didn't move. He waited for the bullet to smash into him. Running feet went past him. He rubbed at his eyes, at last managed to get them part-way open. He saw Pelton's three children squatting beside the saloonman where he lay face down in the street.

Etheridge's three girls stood in a cluster halfway between the schoolhouse and the group in the street, too terrified to come on, afraid to run away. Buck stood on the boardinghouse veranda, calmly and methodically reloading his revolver.

Wagner had holstered his gun. He stood now, big, slow and untroubled. Suddenly Casey hated him for his immense size and power, his monstrous immovability.

Pelton's children were crying, high, thin sounds that were peculiarly Indian, grieving for their father. And Bell looked down at Casey with fury in his eyes, his gun ready.

Casey said wildly, helplessly, "Go ahead, shoot! You're going to be sorry if you don't. Maybe you'll get away with robbing the stage. But I'll come after you if I'm alive. I'll get you if it's the last thing I ever do."

For the first time he saw expression in Bell's empty eyes. Hatred, and ungovernable rage. He waited for the gun hammer to fall.

CHAPTER 5

Wagner's voice was deep, his speech slow. "You need him, Bell. You don't need any of the others but you need this one. Take it easy."

Bell slowly holstered his gun, his eyes showing Casey a burning hate. He toed Casey with his foot. "Get up. Maybe we do need you. But you pull one more stunt like that and it'll be your last." He called to Buck on the porch as Casey was getting to his feet. "Find out which one of those women is the schoolteacher. Tell her to get these damned kids off the street."

Buck went inside, and a moment later came out with Grace Loftus. She wouldn't look at Casey. Nor would she look at Bell. Holding her skirts up to keep them from trailing the dust, she went to where the three Etheridge girls stood trembling. "Go on over to the schoolhouse, girls. I'll be right there."

Grace went over to where Pelton's half-Indian children squatted beside his body. She pulled them to their feet without much gentleness, and shooed them before her toward the school as if they were so many chickens. As they passed by, Casey saw their tear-splotched, bewildered faces. Their dark eyes looked tortured and lost.

Their mother was dead. Now their father was gone, too. Casey knew that nobody in town would take them in because of their mixed blood. The Arapaho would want them, though. Their mother's kinfolk would come and get them as soon as they knew they were alone. They'd be happier with the Arapaho anyway. But with those brown-faced youngsters gone, the town would no longer be safe. Buffalo Wallow would be just another white-man's town, encroaching on Indian land, rich with plunder for the taking. . . .

Grace Loftus disappeared into the school, scurrying the last few feet like a frightened rabbit heading for its burrow. The door slammed behind her and Casey could hear the bolt being shot into place.

She probably thought she was safe, now. She'd find out how safe she was if the outlaws wanted to get into the schoolhouse, Casey thought sardonically. Yet if that bolt gave her a sense of safety, Casey was glad.

Bell's voice pulled his thoughts back to his own predicament. "Come on, Day. We're going after Housman."

Wagner had escorted Etheridge to the porch of the boardinghouse. When Etheridge went inside, the big man returned. He and Bell and Casey trudged on, passing the limp body of Pelton.

Housman was the last one. When Bell had him, he had the town. And when he had the town, he had the stage. Unless Casey could warn them as they pulled in. But Bell had been thorough so far. Likely he'd keep right on being thorough. There'd be something to enforce Casey's co-operation — and Casey knew what it would be; the same thing it had been the last time in Denver.

The hostages in the boardinghouse. They would die if he failed to co-operate. How *could* he warn the stage?

Bell was talking to Wagner. "Housman sure as hell heard all that ruckus. He's liable to be waitin' for us. So watch your step. Keep your gun in Casey's back."

They cut through the lot along the path worn there by Housman and his wife and son, and came to Housman's back door. Casey glanced around. The part of Main Street where the fight had taken place was out of sight.

Bell walked in without knocking. Casey followed, prodded by Wagner's gun.

Marian Housman turned. Her hand went involuntarily to her mouth, her eyes widening.

She was a handsome, full-bodied woman

in her early thirties, with dark hair and eyes. There was always a suggestion of dissatisfaction about the set of her full mouth, Casey had noticed. She saw Casey and began to flush with anger.

Bell said, "Easy, lady. There's a gun in Casey's back."

She looked at Casey. "What is the meaning of this?"

Casey said, "Stage holdup."

"I heard some shots. What . . ." Her anger was fading; fear was taking its place.

Casey said, "Pelton was killed."

Her eyes accused him and he felt anger. What the hell did they expect? Probably they all thought he should have prevented this thing from happening, somehow. When it was over, Grinstead wouldn't consider the difficulties. He'd see just one fact, that Casey had let the outlaws succeed.

Housman's voice came from the parlor. "Marian? What is it?"

Bell spoke in a low tone. "Tell him to come out here."

She raised her voice. "Matt. Come out here." Casey watched the struggle in her eyes, then heard the fright in her voice. "Bring . . ."

Bell's hand clamped over her mouth. The gun in Casey's back prodded harder.

The door opened and Housman came in. His glance took in the scene before him and he started to turn and go back through the door.

Casey saw the look of contempt cross Marian's face as Bell's voice cut the silence like a whip. "Mister, I've got your boy down at the boardinghouse."

Housman froze. Casey thought wryly that Housman had probably turned to go back after a gun, and this wife of his could only think that he had tried to run.

Housman's voice was strained. "What do you mean, you've got my boy?"

"What I said, Mister. He's down at the boardinghouse with some others. Two of my men are there, too. If anything happens . . . if we have any trouble here . . . they'll finish him."

Casey watched Housman's face. Surprise and unbelief registered there briefly, then bewilderment and anger. And then came acceptance, calm acceptance of an unpleasant fact that for the moment at least could not be changed. He looked at Casey. "What do they want?"

"The special coach that's due in here at ten. It's carrying money to a bank in Denver."

Housman was a man of medium height,

slightly built but well muscled and strong for his size. Most men out here lounged when they walked, slumped when they sat. Housman carried himself like a cavalry officer. Casey knew he had fought in the war and had spent a year in Andersonville prison before the end of the war. He also knew, without knowing how it happened or when, that something had broken Housman, so that nothing in life was worth fighting or striving for — not even his wife.

Housman said, with weary acceptance, "What do you want from us?"

Bell said, "Your wife. Then we'll release your boy so he can go to school."

Housman nodded. He glanced at his wife, then at Casey. Casey said, "No use to buck them, Matt. They hold all the cards."

Housman said, "Come on, Marian. We seem to have no choice."

Without speaking, she picked up a shawl from a chair back and went out the back door. Housman followed, then Casey and the two outlaws. Crossing the vacant lot by the path they used coming here, they came out into Main.

Housman saw Pelton's body first, still lying in mid-street. It had the recognizable inertness of death. Housman swung around, anger in his eyes. "Why'd you have to do that? He's got three little kids."

Marian stopped, looked at Pelton, then swung away. Her eyes touched her husband, then swung to Bell. "Who else have you murdered?"

Bell said sharply, "Slack off, lady."

She turned her withering glance to Casey. "They've killed a cowhand from Ramirez' ranch," he told her. "Mrs. Housman. I don't think words will help any now."

From the open window of the schoolhouse up the street, Casey could hear Grace Loftus' and the children's voices singing. It was a hymn Casey recognized: "Onward Christian Soldiers."

Bell herded them on across the street and up the steps to the boardinghouse porch. Marian Housman stepped inside, and her husband followed. Casey, entering behind them, saw the look that flashed between Marian and the cowed Shawcross. The beefy man looked away uneasily.

Mark Housman went immediately to his mother, and had only a half-sullen look for his father. He was white and frightened, but his eyes were steady and there was no tremble in his voice. He said, "Do what they say, Mother, and you'll be all right."

Bell broke in. "Go on over to the school, kid, and stay there. Buck, watch him 'til he

64

gets there."

Mark turned and went out the door. The boy had not looked at his father after that first quick, unfriendly glance.

Bell said, "Buck you and Wagner search the town for guns. Bring 'em back here. We'll throw 'em down the well. Make it fast. It's almost nine already. Bring Etheridge's wife back with you when you come."

Wagner and Buck went out. Buck stood on the porch and watched until Mark reached the school and went inside. Then the pair disappeared from sight.

Bell lounged against the wall, watching the others. Shawcross hadn't moved. The cowpuncher sat in almost the same position he'd been in when Casey had left. Amanda Gooch was up in a chair now, sitting alone. Her eyes were fear-haunted as she looked at Casey. She was probably beginning to realize that her life lay in the palm of her husband's hand, he thought. Maybe she was wishing she'd been a little less despotic toward him.

Lorene sat beside her. Casey's eyes met Lorene's and he was surprised to find them warm and serene. They seemed to tell him that what he had done was enough for her even if it wasn't enough for the others. But her face was pale and when her glance shifted and went to Moya, Casey saw fear come back to her eyes.

He looked at Moya, who sat in a chair tipped back against the wall. There was a toothpick between Moya's lips that he kept rolling back and forth from one corner of his mouth to the other. His eyes, hotly insolent, were on Lorene; they would not leave Lorene.

Casey said, "Bell, if you want me around when the stage comes in, you'd better send that Gila monster outside. If you don't, I'm going to kill him — or try."

The words shifted Moya's glance to him, so filled with virulence and hatred that for a moment his body felt cold.

Bell said to Moya, "Go on out and drag Pelton out of sight."

Moya looked at him. "Go do it youself, if you want it done." He hadn't moved, but there was his hand, resting on his thigh, close to the handle of his gun.

Bell got up deliberately. He walked over to Moya and stared down at him for a moment. He started to turn away, then kicked out suddenly and caught the leg of Moya's chair with his toe. Moya sprawled to the floor with a crash. Before he had stopped moving, Moya's hand yanked out his gun, but Bell's boot came down on his wrist before he could use it. Bell ground his foot against the wrist and Moya grunted with pain.

Gun in hand, Bell stepped back. His tone was unchanged. "Now go out there and get Pelton out of sight."

Moya got to his feet, massaging his wrist with his other hand. He gave Bell, Casey and Lorene searching looks in turn. Then he picked up his gun, holstered it, and went out the door.

Casey said, "That was a mistake, Bell."

Unexpectedly, Bell grinned coldly. "You're too damned smart, Casey. Keep it up and maybe you'll find yourself dead."

Moya came back, retrieved his chair from the floor and sat down. He tipped back against the wall. His face was paler now, his lips were compressed. The expression in his eyes was hidden, deliberately, Casey thought.

Buck and Wagner returned, loaded down with rifles, shotguns and pistols, herding a thoroughly frightened Mrs. Etheridge before them. They went through the kitchen, kicked aside the corrugated cover with a clatter, then dumped their arsenal down the well.

When they returned, Bell said, "All right. Now all you men go on about your business. Etheridge, open the store. Casey, go on down to the way station and catch relief horses for the coach. Shawcross, sit here on the boardinghouse veranda. Housman, hang around with Casey. Maybe you can give him a hand."

He looked at Moya. "Bring your chair over here to the window, so you can watch the street. If anything goes wrong, you know what to do." He went out and returned shortly with a rifle from Moya's saddle boot. "If it looks like we need help, you can help from here."

Moya took the gun and leaned it against the window sill. Then he settled in his chair beside it. Casey, uneasy, sensed in him an expectancy and an eagerness, as though the man only waited for the others to be gone.

Casey went over and stood before him, looking down. He said evenly, "You touch one of these women and I'll stake you out on an anthill."

Moya's eyes taunted him and he didn't speak. Casey struggled with himself a moment. Then he turned away. Never before had he felt for another human being a hatred so consuming, so terrible, so unthinking and reckless. He went outside, feeling contaminated and soiled by his own destructive emotions. He was surprised to realize that he had meant what he'd said about the anthill.

Housman, behind him, said, "Easy, Casey. Take it easy. Another hour and this will be all over."

Casey looked at him bitterly. "For you it will. For the others it will, too. But not for me. That coach is carrying the lifeblood of the Grinstead stageline. If they take it, the line's dead."

"There are other jobs."

"Not for me. Not if I'm standing out there in front of the way station when they come in and I fail to warn them. I'll have a real name, then, for selling out my responsibilities. Who'll hire me with that hanging over me?"

Housman was silent. Casey went on, "And how about the men on the coach? Most of them are friends of mine. How am I going to sleep nights if I let Bell and his bunch slaughter them?"

Housman's voice was steady. "They're paid for taking chances. They knew when they took the job there'd be danger in it." He gestured toward the boardinghouse. "Those women are different. They're not being paid to die for your stageline."

Casey stepped down off the porch. He glanced at the window. Moya was watching him. Moya had a shining sheath knife in his hand that he was whetting on a pocket stone. But his eyes were not on the knife. He was watching Casey, and he was smiling a small, hard smile.

Casey stalked down the street, hands fisted at his sides. Behind him came Housman with Etheridge following. Casey heard Etheridge's key turn in the door of the store.

He glanced northward toward the bluff. He'd be able to see the coach's dust twenty minutes before it rolled into town. Nothing was in sight now.

He found his mind coming back to Housman's words. *"Those women are different. They're not being paid to die for your stage-line."*

Yet suppose he did warn the coach? Suppose the coach crew, once warned, put up a fight and won? Would Moya dare to kill the women over there in the boardinghouse?

There wouldn't be much doubt above it, Casey thought bitterly. These outlaws had already committed two murders, had already invited the hangman's noose. One more or several, would make no difference.

And there was something more. It was plain to Casey that for the man, Moya, cruelty and killing were pleasures in themselves. He would want to savor all he could of them once he himself faced disaster and death.

CHAPTER 6

As Casey passed the telegraph office, he caught a glimpse of Gooch peering at him through the dirty window. It looked to him as if one of Gooch's eyes was swelled almost shut, but he couldn't be sure. Gooch pulled back out of sight too quickly.

Casey could imagine the torment going on in Gooch's mind. In some ways it must be similar to that going on in his own. Gooch had a duty, that of warning law-enforcement officers over his telegraph line. But that duty would be balanced by concern for his wife's safety.

Or did he feel concern? He'd been bullied and nagged for years by that buxom wife of his. He'd been belittled and scorned. Maybe today had presented Gooch with a way out. Casey wondered if the man felt driven to the point of taking it.

Followed by a silent, thoughtful Housman, Casey came to the way station. He went around its north side and into the corral. He took down a rope from the corral fence and walked over to where the horses still milled before the manger.

One by one, he roped out the ones he wanted, and when he had caught them, turned them over to Housman to lead into the barn. When he had enough for the stage, he caught four saddle animals, which he led to the front of the corral and tied. These were to be relief horses for the stage's outriders.

He went back to the barn and helped Housman harness the coach horses. They worked silently and efficiently, and in twenty minutes the job was done. Casey climbed to the loft and looked northward toward the bluff, but he saw no dusty trail in the sky.

He climbed down and with Housman walked to the front of the corral, out the gate and into Main. He looked back briefly at the horses, harnessed and ready beside the fence.

Those relief horses were harnessed to pull the coach, but they'd never pull it. They were only bait, a part of the deceit that had now become Casey's own.

He remembered Moya, sitting in the boardinghouse window, whetting his knife. He remembered Lorene. The way Moya had watched her. He wouldn't kill Lorene. That would be too quick — and easy. It wouldn't satisfy his twisted desires. He'd use the knife, though, somehow. . . .

Revulsion swirled in Casey. He felt helpless, as though he were bound and unable to move. But he *had* to move.

He pulled out his pipe and packed it. Bell, together with Buck and Wagner, had come downstreet and paused before the telegraph office. Bell went in while the other two waited outside. Buck squatted in the street and drew with his finger in the dust. Then he pointed to the way-station loft, and again across the street toward Lorene Mowrey's dressmaking shop.

They got up and started for their places. Then Casey heard an angry shout, and the sound of Bell's voice raging. Gooch came tumbling out of the door to slip and fall in the street dirt.

In the doorway, Bell's revolver puffed powder smoke, and an instant later its report reverberated along the street.

Casey said quickly, "Come on, before they see us! We've got to get to the boarding-house!"

Gooch was dead. His wife would soon be dead too, if they couldn't stop it.

They slipped behind the way station, ran through the corral and came out in the alley. As they ran, Housman panted, "Gooch must have sent off a warning."

Casey nodded, saving his breath. He saw a two-by-four lying in a pile of rubble, snatched it up and ran on.

They rounded the small woodshed behind the boardinghouse, crossed the back yard.

Still running, Casey reached the porch a full fifty feet ahead of Housman, who had paused to look around for a weapon. Casey stopped, and took a few seconds to calm his ragged, noisy breathing. Housman caught up.

Holding the two-by-four in his left hand, Casey eased across the porch. The floor creaked, and the corrugated iron over the well protested audibly.

Casey opened the back door. Maybe he was being a fool. Maybe rubbing out Gooch would be enough for Bell. Maybe he'd let Gooch's wife alone.

But Casey couldn't chance it. It was scarcely more than twenty minutes to stage time. Even now the dust of the stage might be visible up on the bluff or on the road below. Bell could afford no softness now. He'd said Amanda Gooch would die if Gooch sent off a message. If he didn't carry out the threat, his advantage of immobilizing terror would be lost.

There was no one in the kitchen. The door to the dining room was closed. Casey heard a scream, Lorene's voice, and he burst through the door, the two-by-four raised and ready.

Housman came behind him, crowding him. Casey moved a step farther, and heard the sound of a gunbarrel striking a man's skull behind him.

He whirled, swinging the two-by-four blindly. But before he did so, his eyes had taken in the scene in front of him. Moya beside the window, knife in hand; Bell standing at the front door, holding his gun.

Then he turned, and there were Buck and Wagner standing over Housman's unconscious body. Buck held a short gun, Wagner a carbine.

Casey's flailing two-by-four struck Buck's hand and sent the revolver spinning. Buck shouted. Wagner moved in, swinging the rifle. Casey parried with the two-by-four.

A shout sounded behind him, and for an instant he was surprised that he had not felt the bullet's shock. Then Wagner's rifle swung again, this time connecting solidly with the side of his head.

Lights whirled and flashed before his eyes. He was falling. As he fell, he heard another scream, and the sound of a heavy body striking the floor. He struck it himself and knew no more.

He came to, gasping and gagging. Bell stood over him, a bucket in his hand. Bell's voice cold and deadly. "Get up and get down to the way station. The stage is coming."

Casey sat up. He saw Amanda Gooch's bulky body inert on the floor. Lorene was pale, her eyes wide with shock and horror. Marian Housman was kneeling beside her husband, weeping hysterically. Housman was limp and still, his face waxen, but his chest rose and fell and Casey knew he was not dead. In the corner Mrs. Etheridge crouched and whimpered like a hurt animal.

Casey looked up at Bell. He knew his eyes must reveal the monstrous fury he felt. He wanted them to show the promise too, the promise that a time would come when these men would pay.

Bell toed him impatiently. "Come on, come on! Or shall I give Moya the nod?"

Casey got up and staggered toward the front door. The room swam before his eyes. He stopped before Moya. "Remember that anthill I promised you."

Bell gave Casey a push and he went out the door.

Shawcross stood on the porch, his head hanging, his arms at his sides. He did not look up as Casey passed him, but a dull flush stained his neck and face. The man must be broken completely, Casey thought.

Casey walked toward the way station. Behind him, Bell said, "Buck, you and Wagner take your places. You know what to do, but don't do it until you hear my rifle. Then blast away."

Casey didn't even look around, but he could hear Bell's steps close behind him on the walk. Bell said, "Stand in front of the way station like you were waiting, Casey. Wave to them when they roll into town like you always do. Make it good, hero, or you know what Moya will do. I'll let you live — so you can look at Lorene after Moya's through with her."

Casey went cold. It was then that he knew, suddenly, how much Lorene Mowrey meant to him. He couldn't know if she felt the same way about him. He only knew he wanted her beside him.

He wondered how long it would have taken him to realize it if Bell and the others hadn't come today. Maybe he never would have. Chances were he'd have drifted into marriage with Grace Loftus, quit the stageline and gone East. It wouldn't have worked. Good marriages weren't built on shared bitterness. That was all Grace and he had in common.

His gaze lifted, and he saw the dust cloud on the road below the bluff. Five minutes — ten, at the most. Ten minutes in which to decide . . .

A sense of guilt stirred him. Amanda Gooch had died on account of him. Bell had wanted, above all else, to convince Casey he'd do whatever he threatened to do. Casey had been the key, all along.

The cowhand's death, Pelton's, even Gooch's, were apart from Casey, and not his fault. But Amanda Gooch's was. Her death had been Bell's way of showing Casey that he meant what he said.

He came to the way station and stood stiffly before it. Across the street he could see the blue glint of the barrel of Buck's rifle in the half-closed doorway of Lorene's little shop. Above him, in the way-station loft, commanding the whole street, was Wagner. Bell himself had gone into the telegraph office, and Casey noticed that Gooch's body had been taken out of sight. Upstreet in the boardinghouse window was Moya, ready to help if help were needed. And there wasn't a gun in the town except for those the outlaws had.

From the school, faintly, came again the strains of "Onward Christian Soldiers" sung in shrill child voices, led by Grace's fuller one.

Casey looked ahead. He knew now that he'd have to wave the coach in. He had no choice. The men on the coach had, as Housman said, realized the risk involved when they'd taken their jobs. The women back there with Moya could not be expected to die for the Grinstead Stageline.

Casey himself would die. He'd baited the outlaws, fought them. Once the loot was secured, he could hardly expect anything but death at their hands. No use fooling himself about that.

He tried to calculate how long it would take Grinstead to organize a posse in response to Gooch's telegraph message. Denver was over eighty miles away, a two-day ride if the posse were to arrive with their horses in shape for pursuit. And that would give the outlaws a hundred-mile start, or more; they wouldn't care if they killed their horses.

Casey looked northward along the road. He made out the coach, pulled by its galloping teams. He saw the two outriders in front. The two behind were obscured in dust.

He felt like a Judas. Here he stood, bound to wave them into a trap that would mean death to some of them, grievous wounds to the others. And when it was over, they would not curse the outlaws. They'd be cursing Casey.

Within him, for all his ostensible decision, the battle of uncertainty and doubt still raged. Half a dozen times in the next few minutes he wavered. But each time he thought of Lorene, and of Marian Housman, and of Mrs. Etheridge. Of Moya, and Amanda Gooch sprawled on the floor, a threat carried out to constitute a grim warning.

Then the coach rolled into town. Casey raised an arm in greeting. They pulled up before the way station with a deafening rattle of gear, and brakes, and plunging horses.

The driver, intent on his lines, was nevertheless grinning. Pete Etheridge, on the box with the driver, was searching the town for sight of some member of his family, his young face eager and proud. This was his first big run. He was only nineteen.

Outriders stilled their plunging horses, then reined aside to head for the corral. The doors on both sides of the coach opened, and a rifle guard emerged from each.

Casey flinched at the sound of Bell's rifle, flinched as though the bullet had struck him instead of Pete Etheridge up there on the box. Pete half came to his feet, trying to bring his shotgun to bear on something he couldn't even see. The shotgun dropped from his nerveless fingers and fell to the ground. He slid limply to the floorboards and lay there.

The driver tried to shout, to yell his teams into motion, but a bullet from the way-station loft caught him in the throat and the shout was never uttered. The lines fell from his hands and trailed on the ground. He followed them down.

Noise put the teams in motion. A shot from Bell's rifle in the telegraph station brought down the lead horse on the left side and the teams piled up in hopeless, neighing confusion.

All three rifles were barking steadily now. An outrider, halfway to the corral, tumbled from his horse. Another dropped his hastily drawn gun and clutched at his shoulder.

One of the guards who had been inside broke and began to run, rifle held diagonally across his chest, heading for cover from which he could fight back. Then his right leg seemed to collapse under him and he folded to the street.

Casey leaped from the porch of the way station, swung around the heads of the struggling teams and snatched up the shotgun Pete Etheridge had dropped. A bullet, intended for him, slammed into the hip of the horse nearest him and the animal screamed in pain.

But he got the shotgun, swung it around toward the door of Lorene Mowrey's shop and pulled the trigger. Buckshot sprayed the door, but he couldn't tell if it had hit the man behind it or not.

The shotgun was empty now, but halfway across the street lay the inside guard, rifle within reach of his inert hand. Casey ran for it, bending low, weaving and ducking.

Within half a dozen yards of the gun, he felt a bullet tick his sleeve, and he dived for it, sliding in the deep dust of the street. He got the gun in his hands, and rolled, and snapped a shot at Wagner in the loft.

There was still hope, he thought, for besides Casey there were an inside guard and two outriders yet unhurt. But the attack had been too sudden, its results too fearsomely complete. The outriders and the remaining guard inside dropped their guns and raised their hands. Their faces were white with shock and eyes wide as they looked at death.

One of the outriders, hands raised, was knocked from his saddle by a bullet, perhaps aimed and triggered before the man who fired it realized the outrider had surrendered. The other slid off his horse and tried to run. A bullet took a leg out from under him, and he sat down in the street, still holding his hands above his head.

But Casey wasn't giving up. He had nothing to lose. The outlaws had promised him death. He'd rather get it fighting than with his hands raised in surrender. Buck came out of the door of Lorene's shop, and Casey leveled his gun and fired.

He saw Buck go down. Then something struck his head like a blow from a sledge.

He tasted acid in his mouth, tasted the grit of the street, knew that he had failed, knew the sombre aspect of defeat, and then nothing.

Chapter 7

Consciousness returned to Casey, faded again, then came back once more, in waves. Each time he became aware of his surroundings he tried to move, and failed. The terrifying possibility that he was paralyzed crossed his mind.

In his first dim period of consciousness, he heard a volley of shots, the sound of bullets striking flesh. He heard the kicking of horses, their dying struggles, and once heard a windy, sighing, bubbling noise as a bullet cut a horse's windpipe.

It was fortunate that Casey was partly conscious when Moya came over to look at him, to kick him and turn his limp body upon its back. Casey made a grimly determined effort and held his breathing still.

He thought he must surely breathe before Moya turned away, but Moya was hurried by Bell's intemperate, "Moya, damn you, come give us a hand!"

He went away and Casey breathed again with vast relief. He heard them get the box from inside the coach and shoot away its lock. Then he heard the crackle of crisp new yellowbacked bills as they stuffed the bundles of them into gunny sacks.

Lastly, Casey heard Moya's evil, eager voice. "I want that girl, that Lorene. Wait 'til I go get her."

And then Bell's, "Damn you, no! There's plenty of women where we're going. We can't afford to be slowed down, dragging one along."

"Hell, I don't want to take her all the way. I'll leave her in the morning."

"No!"

Moya grumbled, but there was no more discussion of it. And after a few moments,

Casey heard them thunder out of town.

Now he tried to move again. He managed to lift his head, but such waves of nausea and pain hit him that he gave it up.

He heard the moans and the helpless struggling sounds of the stagecoach crew. Nearby, he could hear a horse threshing, and its hoarse and ragged breathing. And scarcely had the hoofs of the outlaws' horses faded from his hearing when he heard another sound — that of swiftly running feet.

Casey turned his head and saw Lorene, white, unnerved by the scene that lay before her eyes.

Her eyes were searching, hopeless, filled with a dread that shocked him in spite of his numbed senses. She began to run again and passed from his sight, then came into his range of vision once more as she rounded the rear of the looted coach.

She saw him then and swayed, so that he thought she was going to faint. But she went on, her lips as colorless as her cheeks, her eyes, still filled with that awful dread, misting with tears.

She knelt beside him and Casey tried to speak. The only sound that came from his throat was a wordless croak.

Quickly, gently, she raised his head to her

lap. With the hem of her skirt she mopped at the bullet furrow that creased his head from forehead to stubborn cowlick.

The pain of it shocked Casey's senses back into clearness. He groaned, and was able to focus his eyes on her face. He said haltingly, "How many dead?"

"I don't know." She was weeping unashamedly.

He said slowly, "Go help the others."

He could hear the other townspeople now, their talk, their movements, the groans of the wounded as they were moved and examined. He heard Grace Loftus' voice. "Faith, take the children and go back to the boardinghouse. Draw water from the well and build up the fire. I want all the hot water you can get on the top of the stove."

Her voice rose again, sharp and angry. "Mr. Shawcross, go with them and remove Mrs. Gooch's body before they go inside. Take her into one of the rooms on the first floor and put her on the bed."

Casey repeated, "Go help the others. They need you, Lorene."

She laid his head gently in the dust. He could hear Mrs. Etheridge weeping brokenly. Then Lorene was saying, "He isn't dead, Mrs. Etheridge. Go home and get some cloth for bandages. Get whatever other things yon can find that you think will help."

Casey could feel his strength returning. He turned his head and saw Marian Housman kneeling beside the inside guard who lay not ten feet away from Casey. Housman, helped by Etheridge, was carrying the wounded unsteadily into the way station.

Casey closed his eyes and with a determined effort of will forced his hands back against the ground and sat up. His head reeled and his vision clouded, but he held on to consciousness grimly until the spasm passed. He slid sideways until he could touch the wounded guard's rifle and, with it, he forced himself to his feet.

Then, for what seemed an eternity, he stood there swaying, gathering his strength, focusing his perceptions, before he began to walk slowly toward the way-station veranda.

Nobody seemed to notice him. He went around the way station. A wave of dizziness struck him and he staggered and fell against the corral fence. The outlaws had been thorough. There was not a live horse left in the corral.

Ironically, there were guns — the weapons of the stagecoach guards — and plenty of ammunition. Casey wobbled across the corral, threading a way through the dead horses. He went along the alley, taking an unusually long time for this, and came at last to the rear of the boardinghouse.

The children, white-faced and terrified, were pumping water from the well. Casey waited patiently until they were through, wishing he had the strength to drag the dead cowpuncher out of their sight.

When they had gone inside, lugging the heavy pails of water, he went to the pump and, working the handle with one hand, stuck his head into its gushing stream. For the second time this morning, its coldness shocked him back to full consciousness.

The oldest of Pelton's half-Indian children, a boy of seven or eight, was peeping at him from the door. Suddenly Casey remembered something. Pelton's kids had a horse, of sorts, staked out in the cattails down by the buffalo wallow.

Casey knew he couldn't walk that far. He tried to smile reassuringly and said, "Tony? That your name, boy?"

The child nodded. Casey said, "Think you could run to the buffalo wallow real fast and bring back your horse?"

The child nodded again, unspeaking. Casey said, "I want to catch the men who killed your father. But I've got to have a horse."

The boy came out through the door. He looked steadily and unblinkingly at Casey for a moment, then set out at a trot for the buffalo wallow. Casey watched him a moment, wondering if this had been wise. Perhaps the kid was so scared he would ride off by himself. Maybe he should have asked Housman or Etheridge to go after the horse.

But all the grownups were busy with the wounded. They wouldn't be concerned with vengeance. Only Casey was concerned with that. And perhaps young Tony Pelton — he was half Indian. . . .

Casey sat down on the edge of the porch. His head ached hammeringly, and he was having trouble with his vision. Sometimes he saw clearly enough, but at other times his vision would blur, or he would see double, the way he got when he'd been drunk.

Once he nearly passed out. He had the feeling that his head was floating above his body, detached and light. Things were as unreal as they were in dreams.

Concussion, he thought. Possible fracture. The bullet that had creased his skull must have packed a hell of a wallop. It must have laid bare the bone of his skull, then glanced off instead of penetrating. If it had struck at a slightly different angle, old Casey would have been killed as Moya thought he'd been.

He had to rest . . . but he had to ride, damn it . . . had to ride.

He laid his head back against a post that supported the roof, and was instantly asleep. He was wakened by a timid hand on his arm.

He opened his eyes and saw little Tony Pelton standing there. Behind Tony was the horse, a swaybacked, ancient paint, gentle as an old dog — and just about as slow.

Casey said, "I'll turn him loose just as soon as I can find another. All right?"

The boy nodded uncertainly. Plainly he was afraid he'd never see the horse again. Casey fought his way to his feet and took the lead rope from the boy.

Out of the yard he went, feeling the boy's dark eyes steadily upon him, down the alley again to the way station. He bridled and saddled the horse, then led him around to the front of the way station, and there dropped the reins.

His mind kept trying to organize the things he would need. Money, first of all. He went through the way station, through the room that was littered with the hurt and the dead, and to the office safe. He opened it and dumped a small drawer of gold coins into a canvas sack. He put the sack in his saddlebags, staggered out and hung the saddlebags on the horse.

Lorene appeared from somewhere and stood close beside him. "What are you doing?"

"Getting ready to go."

"Where?"

"After 'em."

Her hand touched his arm in a quick gesture of protest. "Casey, you can't ride a mile."

He looked at her and went back into the way station. He unbuckled a gun and belt from one of the dead guards and strapped it around his own waist. He was starting out the door again when his knees buckled and he pitched forward on his face.

Pain brought him out of it this time, the raw pain of whiskey in an open wound. It was strong in his nostrils. He heard the tearing of cloth, and then gentle hands were placing a compress over his wound, tying it in place with strips wound all the way around his head.

He forced himself to sit up, and took the bottle from Lorene's hand. He drank, choked, drank again. Grace Loftus was there beside Lorene. "What's this about going after them?" she demanded irritably. "Casey, don't be a fool. There are four of them against you. What do you owe Grinstead?"

There was a sudden and unexpected clarity to his thoughts. He said, "I owe him my best. I owe myself that, too."

"And what about me?" she asked coolly.

Lorene started to get up, as though to leave. Casey put a hand on her arm and restrained her. He wanted no misunderstandings now. "You know nothing but bitterness held us together, Grace," he said. "That's not enough, either for you or for me."

Her mouth thinned angrily. She got up and turned away. He said to Lorene, "Can you find me some food? Can you get me some blankets?"

She hesitated, gauging the determination in his eyes. At last she said gently, "Of course," helped him to his feet, steadied him, then went hurrying out the door.

He moved slowly around the room, staying out of the way, looking down first at one of the guards and then at another. Three of them were dead. Another, shot in the belly, would probably die. Three would live, with luck and care, among them Pete Etheridge. He stopped beside Pete.

He was startled by the venom in the voice that came from behind him. It was

Etheridge's voice, saying, "This is your doing, Casey! You waved them in to their deaths!"

He could have reminded Etheridge that his wife had been at Moya's mercy in the boardinghouse while Casey was waving in the stage. But he didn't. He could have reminded Etheridge that the storekeeper had given Pelton away by his own stupidity, but he didn't do that either. Recriminations never changed anything.

He pushed past Etheridge and went out. Lorene came along the walk, carrying a sack of food and an armload of blankets. Casey took them from her and tied them on behind the saddle. He went over and picked up a rifle, which he shoved into the saddle boot.

He turned to Lorene. Serenity had returned to her face, but she couldn't wholly conceal the anxiety and fear in her eyes. Their expression reminded him of the one he'd seen in the Pelton boy's eyes.

He said, "I've got do to this, Lorene. Can you understand that?"

She murmured in breathless protest, "Nobody blames you for what happened."

"Etheridge does. So will Grinstead. So will a lot of others. And I'll blame myself. I waved them in and they came because they trusted me."

"All right, Casey." But her eyes said it wasn't all right.

He pulled her to him, held her tight against his chest. He said hoarsely, "When I thought of what Moya might do . . ."

She pulled away and looked into his face. Her eyes suddenly brimmed with tears. She whispered, "Come back to me, Casey."

"I'll come back."

"I'll be here until you do. I'll wait, Casey."

A sudden wonder struck him and he asked softly, "How long have you known I was in love with you?"

She smiled at that. "Since this morning. You did a good job of hiding it before that."

"I won't hide it again." He lowered his head and put his lips on hers. She returned the kiss with an abandon that betrayed her, and he knew now why the expression in her eyes had been like that in the Pelton kid's. She was afraid — afraid that she was seeing him for the last time.

He took her hands away from his neck gently and held them. "I'll come back, Lorene."

"Oh Casey, you must," she said fiercely. "You must!"

He pulled away and mounted. "Good-by," he said. He had to leave now. If he didn't, he'd want to sleep. They'd put him to bed and by the time he awoke he'd be too late.

At the edge of town he turned and looked back. She stood where he'd left her, shading her eyes with a hand, looking at him. He raised his own hand, and she returned his wave.

The horse was sluggish, but Casey managed to kick him into a trot. He held him to it, though the jolting made the world swim before his eyes.

The tracks he followed were plain. Later, Casey knew, they would change. They'd split; they'd hide their trail. Or they'd discover Casey was trailing them, and lay an ambush for him.

He'd told Lorene he'd be back, but how could he be sure? Unless he caught the outlaws he couldn't go back. It wasn't just a matter of vindicating himself in Grinstead's eyes. He had to do this for himself. He had to wipe out the memory of death on a prairie-town street. Those men had died because he had stood there and waved them in.

A long trail lay before him. He couldn't guess how long. But it wouldn't be short. Casey knew it wouldn't be short.

CHAPTER 8

The trail led Casey straight south. It was easy to see, easy to follow the first few miles. Clearly the outlaws were concerned at this point only with haste.

Casey clung to the saddle horn, fighting to keep his head clear. Temptation was strong to let the pony slow to a walk, a less punishing gait, but Casey resisted it and held him grimly to his trot.

Time ceased to have meaning. The sun rose to its zenith, began its fall toward the continental divide.

At a sandy, near-dry stream, Casey dismounted, drank deeply, slopped lukewarm water onto his face. The horse sucked nosily at the shallow water a dozen yards downstream.

When Casey rose, dizziness nearly overcame him. He knew, then, that he'd never make it through the day without rest. He tied the horse's reins to his wrist, and lay down on the sandy ground.

He woke with a start to find the sun about two hours farther down the sky. When he stood up his head felt clearer. The dizziness was gone.

He mounted and went on, again urging the horse into his punishing trot.

This was rolling country, covered by a sea of grass that was nearly belly deep on a horse. Small flocks of birds arose as he disturbed them, but they did not go far, circling quickly to alight behind him. It was a treeless country too, for trees cannot live in the dry soil of the great plains unless it be along the bank of some stream or river.

The trail was dimming now as trampled grass sprang back to hide the signs of men who had gone before. Yet still it led directly south, and Casey was able to stay with it. He occasionally lost it, only to pick it up again where the grass was thin and hoof marks visible on the ground.

He envisioned the turmoil which must be taking place in Denver. Grinstead and his top trouble-shooters would have left, probably in company with a United States Marshal, if one was available. The telegraph lines to the east would be buzzing, if the outlaws had not cut them. Casey couldn't remember whether they had or not. Having discovered that Gooch had sent out a warning, Bell probably had not thought it worthwhile.

The sun sank lower and lower in the sky, until it became a flaming orange ball perched atop the western peaks. Casey saw antelope grazing in the evening's cool. He saw buffalo in the distance, and once, riding through a stream bed, he spooked half a dozen mule deer out of it. They bounded away in stiff-legged jumps.

He camped at a stream below a long, low bluff, and picketed his horse out to graze. He should have built a fire and made a hot meal, but his weariness was so great that he only spread his blankets and lay down to sleep. His last waking moment was given over to a prayerful hope that tomorrow he'd feel well enough to travel without stopping at all.

Sun beating into his face woke him in the morning. Rising, he checked his horse and led the placid animal to water. After that, he built a fire with dry grass and buffalo chips, and heated water for coffee.

He drank the hot brew quickly, but nausea was crawling in his stomach so that he didn't try to eat.

He went on, judging he had covered no more than ten or fifteen miles the day before.

The trail was even dimmer now, but Casey's dizziness was gone and his mind was clear. At first, nausea was the only symptom of his injury, but soon there was a pounding pain in his head, and soreness in his wound.

He followed the trail, aware from it that Bell and his companions had slowed their pace. That was good. But until he came upon a camp, he couldn't be sure they had not continued riding through the night.

His thoughts went back to yesterday. Suddenly he remembered something that made his eyes study the land ahead with care. Buck had been wounded by Casey's gun. He had seen Buck fall.

Casey had no way of knowing whether the wound had been a serious one or not. But sometime, probably in late evening the day before, the outlaws would have had to stop and rest their wounded companion and give him some attention.

How far could they have traveled in little more than half a day? Judging from tracks, Casey guessed that they had traveled at a gallop for a good part of it. Then they had slowed. . . . Thirty miles, maybe. Casey's mind settled upon that figure.

Yesterday he'd gone about fifteen himself. Already this morning, he judged, he had traveled nearly ten. Their campsite ought to be somewhere within the next ten miles.

Watchful, Casey rode on with care, though he kept the stolid pony at his bone-jolting trot. He was looking for something else too, a house, a sod shanty, an Indian camp. He

2465052

needed another horse more than anything else right now. If he didn't get more speed and power beneath him, the trail of the outlaws would fade with the passing days and he'd lose them altogether.

Near noon, he came down into a stream bed, riding off a steep bluff. Hungry now, he decided he'd stop here, rest his horse and cook a meal.

An odd uneasiness besieged him as he rode his horse down into the grove of cottonwoods at a bend in the stream. But he shrugged it off, tired and hungry as he was, and drew the pony to a halt. About to slide off, he heard the solid *chunk* of a bullet striking his horse, and felt the animal start and begin to fall. A heartbeat after that, he heard the shouting roar of a gun close by.

The horse seemed to collapse beneath him, and Casey flung himself to the ground behind the horse's back, hoping desperately that he wasn't on the side of the horse toward the shooter.

He'd damned well find out in a minute. . . . He threw a quick glance over his shoulder at the covering trees behind him. Most of them were scrubby, like overgrown bushes. Casey saw nothing, heard nothing but the heaving breath of his dying horse, the faint spasmodic kicking of its hoofs.

Again the rifle roared, and the bullet thudded into the horse before him. Casey's tight nerves relaxed and a little sigh escaped his lips. The dead animal was between him and whoever it was that had bushwhacked him.

It must be Buck. He must have been badly wounded, so badly that he had been impeding the flight of the whole gang. So he'd been left behind . . .

Casey yelled, "Buck? How bad you hurt?"

"Leg." The man's voice was hoarse and tight with pain. "Bone shattered."

Casey yelled, "So they left you! You going to cover their trail after they pulled a stunt like that?"

Buck's voice was fainter. "You've forgot one thing. You're the one shot me, you bastard!"

"Buck, I'm going to kill you. With a leg like that, you're sure to pass out sooner or later. When you do, I'll get you."

No answer came to that. Casey risked poking his head up over the dead horse to look beyond. A rifle cracked and he jerked back, feeling the bullet's wind over his head.

He looked to right and left and behind him. There was no cover for a dozen yards. Behind him the ground rose slightly and he knew he could not retreat without getting killed.

Buck was finished and no doubt he knew it. But if Casey had read the man right back there in town, he was the kind who'd keep Casey pinned here as long as he retained consciousness, or until the night came down.

That would be too damn long. Casey couldn't afford that much delay. He wondered if the outlaws had left Buck's horse with him. They'd have no use for it themselves, and Casey couldn't imagine Buck letting them take it so long as he was in possession of his guns. Unless they had sneaked off while Buck had been asleep . . .

Lying there, Casey remembered Tony Pelton, the way the kid had looked at him as he'd handed Casey the reins of his horse. As though he didn't expect to see the horse again. Casey thought, "I'll send him the best paint pony I can find. A young one. After this is over and done."

He yelled, "Give it up, Buck. I'll fix your leg and leave you here. Someone'll come before long. They'll take you back."

"To a hangman's noose?" Buck's tone was ironic. "Huh uh. This here's all right. I gambled and I lost. But I ain't done yet, by Jesus."

Casey said, "Gooch sent out a message on the telegraph, Buck. That's why Bell killed him. They'll be along and they'll hang you anyway. From a tree right here."

Buck did not reply.

In spite of time's urgency, Casey settled himself as comfortably as he could and closed his eyes. He dozed for half an hour. Then he took off his hat and eased it up over the curve of the horse's back, holding it by the brim. Before it was fully exposed, a bullet snatched it out of his hand and flung it several feet behind him.

He looked at the sky. His nerves were tight, and anger was beginning within him. If Buck kept him pinned here until nightfall, he might never pick up the trail again. Or even if he did find it, it would grow dimmer and dimmer as the days passed, until he'd lose it altogether.

Casey thought of going back to Buffalo Wallow with nothing to show for his pains but Buck. Buck, who would have died anyway, who would have been found by Grinstead's posses, with or without Casey's help.

Casey's hand closed on a rock. He needed a diversion, enough to enable him to rise above the horse's back, enough to give him a chance of spotting Buck's position before

Buck's shot caught him.

But the rock wouldn't do. Buck would see it in the air, would know why Casey threw it.

There had to be another way. Casey lay back and stared at the sky. Far off to his left he saw a hawk, wheeling in the air behind where Buck lay.

Carefully, Casey eased the rifle out of the saddle boot. He waited, hoping the hawk would come nearer. He laid the rock close beside his right hand.

The sun beat down. He began to sweat. He was thirsty, but had no water. He couldn't get to his food, which was in the saddlebags on the horse's sides.

He watched the hawk nervously. It wheeled away, dived, then soared again in wide circles. At last it began to sail nearer the area where the two men lay. It came closer, in huge circles, occasionally beating its wings, mostly gliding with easy grace.

When he was directly overhead, Casey eased his rifle up. The barrel would show above the horse's back, he knew. Perhaps Buck would shoot at it. But the chances were slim that he'd hit such a negligible target.

And when Casey fired, Buck would be unable to resist the impulse to look skyward,

Casey hoped.

Suddenly the hawk dived, almost directly toward Casey. Casey drew a bead, gave the hawk a slight lead, and squeezed the trigger.

Not waiting to see if he scored a hit, Casey flung the rock far off to his right, where it landed in the dry, fallen branches of a dead cottonwood. Then he leaped to his feet, the rifle forgotten, his revolver in his hand.

Panic touched him for a moment as his eyes scanned the tangled underbrush and tall grass before him. He had to catch a movement there. He had to!

For a split second he stood, fighting an impulse to dive back to the cover he'd had behind the horse.

Then his eyes caught a movement and he tensed. His gun muzzle swung toward it, and he made out Buck's form, lying there in the tall grass. He saw Buck's rifle too, its muzzle gaping at him.

He fired, dropped to his knees and fired again.

Smoke billowed from the muzzle of Buck's gun, and Casey fired again. Then he dropped to his belly behind the horse and lay there, sucking air into his lungs in shuddering gulps.

His hands were trembling. He breathed regularly for a moment, then called, "Buck?"

He got no answer.

Suddenly a corner of his eye caught movement in the sky. It was the hawk, wounded, fluttering downward to earth. It crashed noisily into a cottonwood. He heard no other sound.

Suddenly all his patience, his nervousness, his fear were gone. He stood up recklessly, gun held ready. There was still no sound from Buck. He walked to the place where Buck lay and kicked the rifle out of Buck's inert hands.

Casey looked around. Then he began a series of widening circles until he picked up the trail of the four horses coming into the creek bottom. A few moments later he picked up the trail of three horses leaving.

Carefully, patiently, he quested upstream, then down, covering every square yard of the quarter-mile-wide creek bottom. As he did, hope faded, and hopelessness took its place. Buck's horse must be dead. They had finished it off just in case. . . .

He came back to where Buck lay, and there picked up the trail of the man himself, flanked by two who had helped him here. He backtracked this trail, and it led him into an arroyo which branched off the main bed of the stream.

He walked along the dry arroyo for ten minutes. And suddenly he heard, ahead, the stirring and stamping of a picketed horse, beset by flies.

Relief came to him in a flood. He began to run.

The horse was a big black gelding. Sweat was dried on his glossy hide, and caked there with dust. But he was rested now. He looked up curiously as Casey came around a bend in the arroyo, and spooked away to the limit of his picket rope.

Casey pulled the stake and advanced toward the horse, coiling the rope as he went.

This was a good horse, a powerful one. By God, luck hadn't deserted him entirely.

He led the horse back to the scene of the ambush, removed his own gear from the dead paint and put it on the black. He found Buck's saddlebags and went through them, but they were empty. He found a couple of gold eagles in Buck's pocket, and that was all.

He stuffed Buck's revolver into his own saddlebags, along with his bullet pouch and powder flask. Since Buck's rifle was the same calibre and make as his own, he took primers, paper cartridges and bullets from

Buck's saddlebags and transferred them to his own.

He built a fire, heated coffee and ate some of the food Lorene had given him. Then he mounted, and rode out.

Today he had faced a wounded man alone, and only luck had saved his life. Tomorrow, or next week, or next month, he'd face the other three.

But he felt stronger now. He had eaten. His head was clear. His eyes looked out across the vast distance ahead. He urged the horse on in a mile-eating rocking lope across the savage, open land.

CHAPTER 9

He rode hard all the rest of that day, halting only when he could no longer see the ground or the trail he followed. He ate heartily, and then lay down to sleep. Tomorrow he would wake before the dawn, as he always did.

The sky along the eastern rim of the plain was a deep gray line when he opened his eyes. For an instant he lay still, listening to the utter quiet of the land with a growing sense of vague uneasiness.

Scarcely moving his head, he looked around. He saw nothing, no movement of bird or beast. He heard nothing save the restless stamping of his horse's hoofs.

The unease persisted. Looking at his horse, he noticed that its ears were pricked, that it stared steadily at something outside the range of Casey's eyes.

Snatching at the gun which lay beside his hand, he eased himself to his feet. A chill ran down his spine. A half mile away was a file of mounted Indian warriors, heading directly toward the place where Casey was camped.

So far, their keen eyes had not picked him up. A rise of land lay between him and them, so that only his head and that of his horse could have been visible to them. As he watched, they dropped out of sight into a shallow ravine.

Stooping, he snatched up his saddle and ran toward his horse. The animal spooked away, but Casey caught him and flung the saddle to his back. He replaced the picket rope and halter with his bridle, and then led the animal, tight-reined, to the remains of last night's fire.

There was nothing to do but run. He could not guess the temper of the Indians. Even if they were only a hunting party, they wouldn't be likely to pass up the chance to add a scalp to their trophies.

He swung to his saddle, noting that they were still out of sight. If he could get away without being seen . . .

Leaning low over the black's withers, he rode along, keeping to the low ground, keeping that ridge between him and the Indians.

They'd find his camp, no doubt, or his trail beyond it. But perhaps by the time they did, he'd be out of sight.

He found a long arroyo, then turned into it, and rode almost three miles before it petered out. When he looked behind, the Indians were nearly out of sight in the distance.

Still he stayed under cover whenever he could. They might or might not follow his trail when they found it. But they'd certainly pursue him if they saw him.

At last he judged it was safe and lifted his horse again to a run across the plain. He had lost the trail of the outlaws in avoiding the Indians. But he'd pick it up again. He had to.

His horse ran well, breathing easily and sweating little. A good horse, toughened by many miles of riding.

At noon, Casey dismounted and removed the saddle from his horse. He rubbed the animal down with handfuls of dry grass, picketed him out and let him graze. He built a fire and boiled coffee, aware of the danger in this, but also aware that he had to keep up his strength. He cooked and ate the last of the food Lorene had given him. He lay down and dozed briefly before he rose, stamped out the remains of his fire and stowed away his gear.

Aware that other hunting parties might be out, also aware that somewhere nearby was an Indian village, he kept to the sides of ridges, with only his head visible above them at intervals so that he could watch the plain. He sought out the hard ground. Once he rode in a stream for nearly five miles to obliterate his trail.

At nightfall he came to a broad, sandy, near-dry river, flowing, as nearly as he could tell, in a southeasterly direction.

Suddenly, all the irritation of the frustrating day dissolved, for this sandy riverbed offered a solution to the problem which had plagued him ever since he'd been forced to abandon the outlaws' trail early this morning.

He had ridden west of the trail. In the morning he could ride southeast, following this stream and, barring a rain, he could pick up the outlaws' trail where it crossed this bed of sand.

He camped in a small arroyo which branched off the stream. He picketed his horse so that the animal could not climb out to the plain above. He built no fire, since he had no food, but he smoked his pipe before he lay down to sleep, rifle, cartridges and revolver near at hand.

But tonight he did not sleep. Parading before his eyes were Gooch and the puncher from the Ramirez ranch — Amanda Gooch and the others who had died by the outlaws' guns . . .

Grinstead would have reached Buffalo Wallow by now. He knew Grinstead, knew the way the man's mind worked. When Grinstead found Casey gone, he would automatically assume that Casey had been in cahoots with the outlaws. Casey's disappearance would prove it to Grinstead.

To the townspeople he'd argue, "Hell, they beat him up and gave him a bad time just to make it look good. It's just like last time, when he turned a safe full of gold over an' then bleated about bein' afraid they'd kill the girl."

Casey's thoughts ran on bleakly. Grinstead would waste no time. Messages would go out over the wires, alerting law-enforcement officers in every town that had any for a thousand miles. Posters would be printed, giving Bell's and Moya's and Wagner's descriptions, but bearing Casey's photograph. The Pinkertons would be called in.

Probably Grace Loftus was doubting him already. She knew his bitterness; she knew his resentment toward the stage company. It would seem logical to her, therefore, that Casey should choose this way to revenge himself.

He wondered about Lorene. He called up a lingering mental image of her. He thought of her serenity, of the softness in her eyes as she looked at him. He was thinking longingly of Lorene when he went to sleep.

Dawn found him in the saddle. He rode with care, so that no matter what he might encounter, his horse would be strong and ready for it.

He had no way of knowing where the Indian encampment was. It might be upon the banks of this watercourse along which he rode.

He watched the sandy bed of the stream with careful eyes. Once he crossed the trail of several horses; they were unshod and small, so he knew the tracks had been made by another hunting party.

Deer, frequenters of stream beds because of the abundance of browse, bounded away from him as he rode. He was hungry now, ravenously so. But he dared not kill a deer, knowing the shot might be heard by Indians.

Near noon, he finally cut the trail of Bell and his men. His spirits rising, he turned south again along the fading trail. He urged his horse to a trot. It was the fastest gait at which he could make out the dim tracks of the outlaws.

He found their noon camp, and he knew then that he was a full day behind. He knew also that from now on their lead would not increase.

Slowly the sun slid down the sky. Slowly Casey traveled across the empty, endless grass.

At sundown, he rode to the top of a bluff from which he could see miles in every direction. He studied the plain with minute care for a full half hour, but he saw nothing — no smoke, no dust, no moving creature save for a dozen antelope in the near distance, and a herd of buffalo upon the horizon.

He had to eat soon. Tonight it might be safe to risk a shot. He hastened along a course which would bring him to the buffalo herd.

It was nearly dark when he came upon them, but in the fading light of the sky, he lined his sights on a calf and pulled the trigger. The calf fell and the herd thundered away, to stop a short distance off.

Casey skinned and gutted the calf by feel in the darkness, then hoisted the dripping carcass to the back of his horse. He rode, then, for a full five miles to the point where he had abandoned the outlaws' trail. Here he built a fire and picketed his horse out to graze.

He broiled chunks of the meat and ate voraciously. When he was full, he killed the fire and moved on again in the darkness for half a mile. Before retiring, he propped the calf carcass up against the saddle, abdominal cavity up, so that it would cool out during the night.

In the morning, he again risked a fire, and ate broiled buffalo meat until he could not stuff down another mouthful.

His strength was returning fast. His battered face was healing, and his head wound was solidly scabbed so that now he was able to remove the bandages.

In midmorning he found a spot where the outlaws had encountered a party of eight Plains Indians. There had been a brief fight, and the Indians had retired. Bell and Moya and Wagner had gone on, hurrying. A spot of blood on the ground told Casey that they had either killed or wounded an Indian, unless one of their own number had sustained a wound.

The afternoon clouds, which had hung all day over the western mountains, began to drift out across the plain. They were dark clouds, and from their rims wavering sheets of rain fell down upon the land.

Anger gripped Casey. He urged on his horse until the animal was traveling at a gallop. Rain sweeping across the plain would blot out the outlaws' trail.

If they were playing it smart, they'd change course as soon as the rain began, to throw off possible pursuit.

Slowly the clouds spread across the face of the sun, on eastward until they covered the entire sky. The rain came, visibly sweeping eastward in the distance, gentle at first, but increasing in intensity until the ground ran with it, until each small gully was filled to overflowing with a muddy torrent.

The trail was blotted out, but Casey went stubbornly on, choosing a course which men headed south might logically be expected to follow. But frustration was beginning to build in him; he was beginning to doubt his own capabilities.

He was a fool, he told himself. He had lost them. They'd find a town and separate, each with his share of the loot. With no trail to follow, Casey would have to try to follow them by questioning the inhabitants of this sparsely settled land.

And in the towns, everyone's hand would be against him. Grinstead would have sworn out warrants long before now. The far-flung organization of Allan Pinkerton would be on Casey's trail.

Casey Day had lived with bitterness for a long time. Well, he would live with it some more. Yet he refused to admit the possibility that he might fail. Eventually he would catch them, one by one. Bell, Moya, Wagner. When he did, he would avenge himself. And all of those others who had died at their hands, they would be avenged too. . . .

The clouds passed, and again blue sky showed over the distant peaks. The cloud mass drifted on eastward, leaving an ever-widening expanse of blue in its wake. The sun came out again, to lay its warming rays upon the chilled and dripping land.

The torrents in the arroyos slackened and stopped. Casey's clothes began to dry under the steaming heat of the sun as he traveled on blindly. Then his spirits lifted as he crested a long rise of land and saw a tiny sod shanty before him in the distance.

Bell might have stopped here for the night. If the outlaws' food supply was running low, as it might well be, they could have stopped here to replenish it. . . .

Casey rode down the grade toward the shack at its foot. A stream wound from left to right here, looping and curving like the coils of a snake. Smoke rose from a tin chimney in the roof of the shack.

A tiny corral held a pair of horses. A plow lay on its side beside a half acre of sod that had been turned by it. A stack of wild hay reared up behind the house, three times its height.

Casey wondered briefly at the stark courage of the people who had built this shack. Here they were, calmly taking land which the Indians claimed — calmly going about the tasks of plowing and settling, as though they were under the guns of a powerful fort.

He was two hundred yards from the shack when the shot rang out. He saw the puff of powder smoke, heard the whine of the heavy slug.

He was off his horse before the animal had time to spook away. Down on his belly in the tall grass.

His blood raced and his head began to pound. He'd found them, by God! All he had to do was wait until night. Then he could close in on them. Then he could start making them pay — in blood.

Chapter 10

The tall grass was still wet from the rain, but it was steaming hot even so. Casey watched his horse which had cantered away as Casey left the saddle. Now it was grazing calmly fifty feet away.

As Casey watched, he heard a nicker from the corralled horses down at the shack. Casey's black lifted his head and answered, then trotted down the slope toward the cabin.

Casey held his breath, waiting for a shot to ring out. It would be damned easy for whoever was shooting at him to kill his horse and so put him afoot. With that done the outlaws could leave in early darkness, knowing that the best mount available to Casey was one of the plow horses in the corral.

But he heard no shot, and after a few moments the sound of his horse's hoofbeats faded.

He lay quite still, breathing slowly and evenly so as not to stir the grass in which he lay. And he waited.

He had left the saddle instantly when the shot rang out. The outlaws had no way of knowing Casey was alive. Perhaps they'd think they'd killed him. If so, they might come out to investigate.

No one came. Casey began to itch intolerably from the moisture and the heat. Gradually the sun sank toward the horizon.

After almost an hour, Casey risked moving. He crawled slowly and carefully, hoping the movement of the grass would not betray his progress. When he had gone a hundred yards, he raised his head to look.

He saw nothing he hadn't seen before. The shack lay as though unoccupied, except for the wisp of smoke drifting away from the stovepipe. The windows, high and narrow, were covered with oiled hide which permitted light to enter, but which could not be seen through. The door was opened a crack, but Casey could see no one looking out.

From this angle he could see the west side of the haystack, which had not been visible to him before. Parked there was the nester's wagon, its canvas top in shredded tatters.

The outlaws' horses must be behind the haystack. There they'd be hidden from any who might come along the outlaws' back trail. If they were behind the stack, they had neither seen nor heard Casey's horse, nor he them, for the black now stood beside the corral, reaching over the top rail to poke his muzzle toward the plow horses.

Casey wished mightily that he had his rifle. He could see it sticking out of the saddle boot on the black down by the corral.

He crawled again, this time heading directly downhill toward the nester's cabin. He wondered how the nester and his family were faring. In all probability they were huddled inside the cabin under the outlaws' guns.

Perhaps only one of the outlaws was holed up down there. Casey recalled the blood he had seen on the ground back there where Bell and the others had run into the Indians. Maybe the other two had gone on, leaving their wounded comrade behind.

Time dragged, became an endless thing. If one had been left behind, it meant the other two were going on, putting more and more distance between Casey and themselves.

Casey raised his head and looked again. This time he saw the blue muzzle of a rifle poke its way through the doorway. He dropped back and the gun roared. The slug whined away overhead, to ricochet off the slope some distance behind where Casey lay.

After that, Casey kept his head down and lay still. He knew he had no chance of reaching the cabin alive in daylight.

He dozed, while the sun beat down against him and made him sweat. He slept on after it had dropped low enough so that it no longer shone directly upon him. He woke with a start as the last glow of it faded from the piled up rain clouds on the eastern horizon.

Waiting became doubly burdensome now that the time for action was close. Casey's muscles drew tight.

Dusk came slowly. Even before it did, Casey was moving, crawling through the grass along a course which would carry him around the slope to the side of the cabin.

He reached it in the last gray light of day, and after a quick look, rose to his feet.

He stood still for a long time, looking downward until the shape of the black there beside the corral became so indistinct that he couldn't be sure he was actually seeing it. Satisfied then, he walked down the slope, careful to make as little noise as possible.

There was no sound. He walked on, unchallenged, and came up to the side of the cabin in complete darkness. He halted momentarily to listen. Hearing nothing, he eased around the corner and faced the dark doorway.

He drew his gun. A chill crawled along his

spine. There should have been some noise — something besides the shots — a warning to leave, a threat, a shouted insult.

In the darkness he could not tell whether the door was open or closed. Keeping his back to the wall, he eased toward it, feeling along the wall with his free hand. He felt the jamb and then the door, which was slightly ajar.

Suddenly, then, Casey flung himself against it and charged into the darkened interior. His hand encountered the cold steel of a rifle, and he seized it, wrenched it loose, and flung it aside blindly. He heard then a sharp cry of surprise and terror; it was a woman's voice.

He charged across the room unseeing, only knowing he must get away from the door and the faint square of light the stars made against the blacker interior of the room.

He ran into a table and sent it crashing to the packed dirt floor; dishes smashed and a pan banged against the stove in the far corner of the room. The woman began to moan hysterically.

Casey stopped, holding himself utterly still, stifling even the sound of his breathing.

Gradually he became aware of another

sound beside the moaning of the woman. It was the stifled breathing of another person, broken by an occasional sharp intake of breath.

Casey cocked his gun. In the silence, the sound seemed as loud as a shot.

He dared not move. He scarcely dared to breathe, lest the sound give him away. He had located two people; the woman by the door, and the other, the one whose breathing was so forcibly restrained.

There should be more than two — a man, the nester, at least one of the outlaws, perhaps more than one.

Straining his ears, he gradually became convinced there could be no more than two. He found a match in his pocket, struck it with his left hand and held it aloft while his eyes ran like lightning across the cluttered, tiny room.

He saw the woman crouched by the door, her eyes like those of a terror-stricken animal. He saw a girl huddled on a bed.

The match went out. Casey struck another and the light of this one showed him the body of a man upon the floor.

His held breath sighed out. He crossed the room to the lantern that hung from the low ceiling and lighted it.

The girl tried to draw farther into the

corner, her dread-filled eyes clinging to him. The woman by the door tried to reach the rifle, which her questing eyes had located in the lantern's first light.

Casey crossed to her and put his foot on the gun just as her hand touched it. He said, "Good Lord! Were you doing all that shooting?"

He got no answer. They watched him, their eyes unchanging. He had the queer feeling that if he should as much as touch either one of them, both would probably burst into hysterical weeping. He picked up the rifle and crossed to look at the man.

This, he guessed, was the husband of the older woman, father of the girl. His face bore the marks of brutal fists. He had been shot in the chest. The front of his shirt was soaked with blood. His body was cold.

Casey swung to look at the woman, then at the girl. One of the girl's eyes was black, nearly swelled shut. Blood had trickled from a corner of her mouth and dried on her chin. Her mother had a purple bruise on her cheekbone and her lips were puffed and swollen.

Casey sat down on a crude bench. Making his voice as soft and gentle as he could, he said, "I'm not one of them. I'm chasing them. I won't hurt you, either of you."

He got no answer from either. He tried again, keeping his voice patient. "Your man needs burying. Then you've got to leave."

Panic touched the woman's face. It was not a pretty face, nor a strong one. Yet, Casey could tell, it had once been pretty; once smiles had come easily to this woman's lips.

Probably she had looked like her daughter. The girl would be very pretty indeed with her hair combed, with terror and the shame erased from her face.

Anger hit Casey hard, but he said again, patiently, "You've got to leave. You can't stay out here alone. I'll bury your man and then . . ." He stopped. He'd been going to say he would see them off for the nearest town.

Wearily resigning himself, he said instead, "I'll take you to Bent's Fort. You'll be safe there. You can travel back East with one of the Army's wagon trains."

The woman spoke for the first time. "No!"

Casey looked at her. "There's Indians all around you, Arapahos and Cheyennes. What beats me is they let you stay this long."

"We'll stay," the woman said stubbornly.

Casey got up. "Still figure I'm one of them that did this to you?"

The woman shook her head hesitantly.

"Feel up to scraping together some grub?"

She nodded.

"Then suppose you do that. Tell me where the shovel's at and I'll start digging your man a grave. Any special place . . . ?"

She shook her head wearily. "There's a shovel at the back of the house." Her voice was tense.

"Need chips for the fire?"

"Bessie'll get them."

Casey looked at the girl, still crouched motionlessly on the bed, and then went out the door. His hands and knees were shaking, and the skin of his face felt tight-drawn and cold. He thought of Moya, and he realized that his hands were clenched tight.

He didn't know exactly what had happened here last night, but it wasn't hard to guess. He found himself thinking of what he'd do to Moya, if he ever got his hands on the man. For the first time in his life he was seeing some sense in the kind of things Indians did to captives. Simple killing wouldn't be enough. . . .

Casey found the shovel and went out behind the house where the hill began. Working in faint starlight, he began digging a grave. He worked hard, as though intensive effort could ease the tension that outrage had built in him. He began to sweat, but he kept going, and gradually muscles and nerves relaxed.

He went down four feet, deep enough, he guessed, for a grave that would be unrecognizable as such in a couple of years. Then he went back toward the house.

He heard the girl weeping brokenly before he reached it. He stumbled over a broken wagon wheel and kicked it savagely. It hurt his foot, but the pain felt good. He began to curse softly.

He went in. There was a skillet on the stove filled with frying meat. The woman's face was still and cold, but once her eyes touched her daughter's huddled form on the bed and softened helplessly. When she looked at Casey, they were bright with tears.

Casey spoke to her. "My name's Casey Day. I work for the Grinstead stageline. An outlaw named Bell and his bunch took a hundred and fifty thousand dollars off the stage three days ago and killed several people doing it. I've been trailing them. It was them that were here. I'm sure of it."

He righted the table, and a bench, and sat down. The woman, who said her name was Mrs. Tilton, gathered up the scattered dishes and began to wash them in a pan full of hot water that simmered on the edge of the sheet-iron stove. Then she set them out on the table.

Casey noticed that the man's body had been wrapped in blankets. He went over and lifted the man in his arms. The woman picked up the lantern and followed him out wordlessly. Behind them the girl began to weep again.

He carried the body to the grave and laid it down. Then he took the lantern from the woman and went back to the shack. She followed him wordlessly.

Inside, the woman's voice grew harsh. "Bessie, quit that and git up here to the table. Starving yourself ain't going to make you feel any better."

Bessie sat up, wiping her reddened eyes with the back of her hand. Obediently she came and sat down across from Casey, keeping her eyes downcast.

Casey said, "Forgetting last night isn't going to be easy. But you'll have to do it. You keep thinking about it and . . ."

His voice trailed off and they didn't respond. The woman filled his plate, then Bessie's and her own. Casey ate; the woman managed a couple of mouthfuls, but the girl wouldn't touch her food. When Casey was finished, Mrs. Tilton went to a small, leather-bound trunk and took out a Bible. Casey got the lantern and followed her outside. The girl came after him, face white, shoulders sagging.

He lowered her husband's body into the grave clumsily with his lariat. Then he stood with head bowed while she read from the Bible in a wavering, uncertain voice. The girl, Bessie, began to sob hysterically.

When the woman had finished, Casey said, "Go back to the house and pack your things. I'll finish up here."

They went away. Casey could hear their voices, the woman's trying to calm the hysterical girl, the girl's rising and frantic: "What if I have a baby, Ma? What'll I do? What'll I *do?*"

They worked until after midnight. When they were finished, the house was bare, the wagon loaded with their possessions. By lantern light, Casey checked its running gear and greased the axles. The rig should make it as far as Bent's Fort, which could not be more than a couple of days away.

Casey unrolled his blankets and lay down to sleep beside the wagon. By the time he had got the two women to Bent's, the outlaws' trail would be obliterated by time and rain. From here on, he would have to track by instinct and feel, by guesswork and logic, by trial and error.

He lay and stared at the stars. His original purpose had been to vindicate himself in

Grinstead's eyes. Now, he realized, that purpose had become unimportant to him. Unreasoning hatred, a consuming desire to exterminate the three, had taken its place. He thought of Lorene, tried to recall her face in his memory, but he could not.

He guessed the outlaws might be heading for Bent's Fort. Their direction indicated the probability, and there were few other places to which they could go in this direction. But from Bent's Fort, where? To Santa Fe, maybe . . . to Taos . . . to Texas . . . Or they might split up and go in three directions. If they did, he'd have his work cut out for him. . . .

He tried to force himself to relax and go to sleep. But he could not. His mind kept on weighing his chances, and they kept looking dimmer. . . .

He finally slipped into a troubled doze for a while, but he was up at dawn, harnessing the two horses to the woman's wagon.

He unwrapped the calf carcass of buffalo and cut off some steaks. He rewrapped it and put it back on his horse. It would not keep long now. He'd forgotten to hang it out the night before.

He carried the steaks into the house and waited, smoking, while the woman cooked them. The girl's face showed no signs of weeping this morning. She was, instead, oddly still and her face was expressionless. Her eyes looked at Casey seemingly without memory or recognition. She could have forgotten everything — the outlaws, her father's murder, her own brutal experience, the reason for leaving.

When the meal was over, Casey went out and stood by the wagon, holding the reins of his black in his hand.

He waited, concealing his sharp sense of impatience, while the woman and her daughter walked to the grave, while they knelt and prayed.

They came then, and mounted the wagon seat. The girl's face was still blank, the woman's was hard and grim. She drove the wagon away to southward without once looking back.

CHAPTER 11

Casey accompanied the Tiltons all the way to Bent's Fort, which now, in its third location, was a log stockade, a hundred feet square, at the mouth of the Purgatoire. It was but a short distance from the new Fort Lyon which Casey carefully avoided on the possibility that somehow word of the holdup might have reached it. He guessed that the outlaws had avoided it too.

Mrs. Tilton, with Bessie beside her, drove her wagon into the stockade and Casey reined in beside her. The blank numbness seemed to have faded in Bessie. Mrs. Tilton looked at Casey now, and for the first time he saw beneath her hard exterior. "I wish I'd put a marker on Sam's grave."

He said, "I'll do that on my way back."

"I thought you weren't going back."

"Not right away, I'm not. But I'm going back."

He took out his money pouch and gave her a hundred dollars in gold. Before she could protest, he said quickly, stretching the facts, "This belonged to one of Bell's bunch that died before he reached your place. It isn't mine and I don't want to keep it."

She closed her hand on the gold, the extremity of her need pitifully clear in this action.

Casey looked at the girl. "You try and forget what happened. Once you get back East, you'll find it easier. There'll be so many young men courting you . . ."

Her voice was bitter. "Who'd want me now? When they know . . ."

Casey said logically, "They won't know unless you tell them. After all, it isn't as though you'd done something wrong."

He turned away. Mrs. Tilton called a good-by. "Thank you for your help," she said gravely. "I don't know what we'd a done . . ."

Casey swung his head. "You keep after that girl. What happened shouldn't be allowed to ruin her whole life."

"It likely won't," Mrs. Tilton said. "She's young and it seems bad now, but she'll get over it."

He held still, and watched them drive away toward the center of the stockade. They were safe now; the responsibility was lifted from Casey's back. Either they'd travel East with the traders or go along with an escorted Army train. They had left something with Casey. It was something that he knew would make him all the more implacable when he caught up with Bell and Moya.

Inquiring, he learned that three men had gone through two days before, stopping only long enough to buy supplies. Then he rode out, heading southwest up the Purgatoire.

Bell had a good two-day lead. Now Casey had to give up following their trail if he expected to catch them at all. Now he must try to anticipate their movements.

They wouldn't head East. In that direction lay Army forts, Fort Mann and Fort

Larned, both on the Arkansas. Either or both of the forts might have received word of the holdup. If they had not, it was certain that both Council Grove and Westport, further eastward, would have.

To westward lay only mountains, slow going and devoid of settlements for several hundred miles, land that was populated only by Utes and across which white men dared not go unless accompanied by a strong party.

Yes, south would be their most likely escape route. To southward was Santa Fe, Taos, Mora and Las Vegas, to say nothing of the smaller settlements where gringo gold would buy anything, even safety from the pursuing forces of the law. And east from Santa Fe lay the vast Texas panhandle, where a dozen men could lose themselves with ease.

In turning up the Purgatoire, Casey gambled on this reasoning. If he was wrong, it meant he would lose the outlaws for months. Perhaps forever.

His clothes were gray with dust and stiff-caked with sweat. His beard, now a week old, gave him a hard, grim look that was heightened by the coldness in his eyes, the intentness of his whole demeanor.

Night came down before he had gone a

dozen miles from the Fort, and he camped. He picketed his horse out to graze. He bathed in the stream and ate the last of the buffalo calf, which was not only dried out, but overripe as well. Then he rode out in darkness; he could travel by night using the river as a landmark. Just before dawn he halted, staked out his horse again, and slept a couple of hours. Afterward he went on without eating.

The country was rising now, as he drew ever nearer the divide to the west. He could see the snow-clad Spanish Peaks in the distance on his right. He passed through an occasional stand of cedar or jack pine, but he saw no game.

So in midmorning, when he sighted an Indian village ahead, he did not detour, but headed straight for it. If he could trade for some dried buffalo meat, he'd be better equipped for a fast trip to Santa Fe, unhampered by the need to hunt.

The village was laid out in a semicircle, facing east. From the tipis, Casey knew it was a village of Arapaho. He hoped they were friendly. If they weren't, he'd find out soon enough to cut and run.

The dogs began to bark while he was yet a hundred yards from the first tipi. It should have been a signal for people to appear, to cluster and stare at him curiously. But no one appeared.

An odd uneasiness possessed Casey. Again he considered detouring, but this time subbornness got hold of him and kept him on his course. He saw a lone Indian boy off beyond the village with the horse herd, which seemed overly small for the size of the village. Other than that, Casey saw no one.

He rode in, and an old man stepped from a nearby tipi and regarded him somberly. Casey held out his hand, palm toward the old man. He received no answering sign, but dismounted anyway, driven by a rising impatience.

This near to Bent's Fort, the Indians should be used to money, so Casey took a gold coin from his pouch and held it up between thumb and forefinger. He said, "Pemmican," and went through the motions of eating something from his hand, then rubbed his belly with a circular motion.

Instead of replying, the old man turned toward the village and shouted something in a cracked, reedy voice.

From the tipis came an assortment of old men, women, girls and young boys, all of whose eyes held the same dislike and hostility Casey had seen in the old man. The old one spoke to them in Arapaho. Casey understood only enough of it to know that the words were inflammatory. Suddenly a stone struck the side of Casey's head. He almost fell. Another stone struck his back. The horse tried to rear, but Casey held to the reins and swung the horse between himself and the Arapaho villagers.

They were shouting at him, caught up with their own violence, but they held back to stone-throwing range.

Anger boiled up in Casey. He shouted, "I'm not one of 'em, damn it. I hate 'em as much as you do!"

Rocks still hailed around him. A couple of times he heard the odd, hissing sound of an arrow, accompanied by the twang of a bowstring.

A thrown tomahawk struck his horse on the rump, and the frightened animal dragged Casey half a dozen yards before Casey could pull him to a halt.

Casey would have mounted then, but surprisingly, the old man shouted at the crowd and the stoning stopped. Then the old man said, in halting English, "Come, I will show you what the three evil ones have done to us."

Casey hesitated. It could be a trick to get him separated from his horse, but he didn't think it was. He tied the horse to a tipi pole, exposed by the raised buffalo-hide covering. Then he followed the old man, hand close to his gun.

The old man led him to a tipi at the far end of the village. The crowd followed, jabbering excitedly among themselves. The old man entered and held aside the flap for Casey. Casey went in.

There were two bodies on the floor, one of a young girl, one of an old man. The faces of both bore the marks of fists, Moya's probably.

Casey went back outside, an angry sickness crawling in his belly. The old man said, "Our warriors are out hunting, for game is scarce. When they return, they will catch and kill these three. The girl is Nata-cea, the wife of Haaxabaani, whom your people call Red Wolf."

Casey asked, "Can you give me some meat?"

"No! You go. You go far. Our warriors will be thirsty for white blood."

Casey walked back to his horse. He mounted and rode away at a gallop. Behind him the people watched him stolidly.

Casey's hatred for the three outlaws had become like a nausea in his stomach. It was a pressure in his head; it was a dryness in his throat and a trembling in his hands. It grew like a grass fire sweeping the dry plain.

He didn't know when the village warriors would return. He knew when they did they would take the outlaws' trail.

And he would not be cheated, either by the Indians or by Grinstead who must now be close behind.

He rode all day, pushing his horse mercilessly. That night he camped on the near side of Raton Pass, being careful to draw off the road for half a mile before he did.

In the morning, he moved on with the dawn. He went out of his way to avoid Dick Wooten's toll station on the pass. He was sure of the direction the outlaws had taken now, and he didn't want Wooten telling Grinstead that Casey had been so close behind.

Now he rode in three-hour spurts through day and night, allowing an hour between each one to rest his horse. Rabbits, killed and hastily broiled, kept him half fed. In Mora, he found a cantina where the outlaws had stopped for a meal. He ate wolfishly himself, then quickly traveled on.

And at last, of an evening, he rode into the narrow streets of Santa Fe.

He put up his horse at a public corral, though it was only for a few hours. "Give him some grain and rub him down," he told the Mexican hostler.

The man looked at him blankly. Casey knew no Spanish, so he led the animal inside and found the grain. He measured it out carefully, not wanting the horse to become heavy with it and unable to travel. He grabbed a sack and began to rub the horse down.

The Mexican said, *"Le entiendo! Me savvy,"* and took the sack from him.

Casey went out and wandered uptown to the plaza. He inquired at La Fonda, the inn at one corner of the plaza, for the outlaws, but was met with blank stares as he described them. Afterward he went out and began to make the rounds of the cantinas, inquiring in each one.

At last, he found one where the outlaws had been two days before. No one knew where they were now, though, or which way they'd headed. Casey had to presume they had left the town.

Discouragement touched him. What if they had split here? It was the logical place for a split. It would be a formidable task to pick up their separate trails.

He went back toward La Fonda, knowing with vast impatience that he could do nothing until morning. He needed supplies, for the trail ahead might be long. And it would be better to wait for daylight because the inhabitants of this land were wary of those who came in the night. Only by questing and questioning would he pick up any trail at all.

There was a band playing in the plaza. The night air was tangy with the fragrant cedar smoke of supper fires, sharp with the smell of red peppers which hung in clusters on the walls of every house.

Girls, accompanied by their duennas, were beginning to parade around the plaza. Young men paraded in the opposite direction and ogled the brightly garbed girls.

Somewhere, a guitar strummed pleasantly, and a liquid male voice sang. Casey knew it would have to be a song of love.

He halted on the gallery of the Palace of Governors, leaned against a supporting pillar and shaped a smoke. His beard was beginning to itch and he scratched at it absently.

He was uneasy. Grinstead and his posse hadn't caught up with him yet, probably because Casey had pressed his horse so hard between Raton Pass and here, but tonight's delay might well be fatal. If Grinstead arrived during the night and caught Casey here . . .

The old man would overlook no bets. He'd have Casey slapped into the adobe-walled jail so fast Casey wouldn't know what happened. And he'd keep him there pending capture of Bell and the others until he rotted, if necessary.

A hundred and fifty thousand dollars. Every time Casey thought of it he whistled to himself. It was an unheard-of haul, even in this land where robbery was common-place. News of the staggering amount would travel across the country like a tornado, by word of mouth. It would give the land's lonely inhabitants something to talk about, American and Spaniard alike.

A subject for talk . . . and perhaps an object for their greed. It would be remem-bered that Casey, obviously no lawman, had been asking questions. His description of the outlaws would be remembered long after he was gone. And Casey himself would become as well known as the outlaws them-selves.

Casey shrugged his shoulders and headed for La Fonda to rent a room. Suddenly he heard a meadow-lark trill. For just an instant he halted, while surprise registered in his mind. Then he whirled.

Boots pounded along the gallery behind him — in front of him. A man cursed in

English. A voice, Grinstead's voice, said disgustedly, "A meadowlark, and at night! Jesus!"

Casey's gun was out of his holster, but Grinstead's harsh voice rumbled at him from the darkness, "You going to add killing to the score against you, Casey? You want to hang?"

Casey sprinted for the street. A shot banged out. Three horses came pounding across the plaza toward him. He swerved, heading back toward the shadowed gallery. An alley yawned ahead.

He collided violently with a man and the two of them went down in a tangle. The man swung awkwardly with his gun and the barrel grazed Casey's head. Casey gained his feet and then several of Grinstead's posse were on him, bearing him back and down. He fought wildly. Blows rained on his body. He heard the horses again, then Grinstead's bellow, "Let 'im up, damn it! I got a gun on him. If he runs, I'll blow his guts out!"

The men got up, one by one. Casey struggled to his feet. He was herded and shoved along toward the lighted windows of La Fonda. Pushed into the lantern-lit courtyard, he found himself surrounded by Grinstead and his posse.

Grinstead was a big man, not as tall as Casey, but broader and thicker. His jaw and jowls were covered by a neatly trimmed beard. His nose was flattened, broken long ago.

His eyes, partly hidden by shaggy gray brows, were as hard and cold as diamonds, and as bright. He was partly bald, but the rest of his hair was the same steel gray as his eyebrows, and coarse as wire.

His voice was like a whip. "So you threw in with them again!"

Casey looked at the man. Anger gripped him. "If I threw in with them, why do you figure I'm chasing them?" he growled.

"To get your split. What else?"

"Got your mind made up, haven't you?"

Grinstead moved like a rattler. His fist smashed into Casey's mouth. Casey staggered back, recovered, and wiped the back of his hand across his bleeding lips.

Grinstead snarled. "You waved in the stage! You damned Judas, you waved them in to the slaughter!"

Casey didn't answer. It was no use. Grinstead was unshakable. Nothing Casey could say would change him.

Grinstead walked over close to Casey. His eyes were virulent, savage. He said, "Damn you, you've ruined me, you and the four you dealt with!"

"I didn't deal with them, Grinstead."

"Well, we got you and that's better than nothing. Now tell me where they're going."

Casey shook his head. "I don't know. What I do know is I'm going where they're going. It's not the same thing."

"You're going nowhere," Grinstead said harshly. "All right, boys." He raised his voice. "Let's put him away."

CHAPTER 12

They took him outside the town, up a long grade to the old Spanish prison, which was still used as a jail by the comparatively recent conquerors of the territory, the Americanos.

The formalities of charge and incarceration were brief. Casey was taken to a barred, stone-floored cell and the door slammed behind him. Afterward, he watched through the tiny window, watched Grinstead and his men ride down the road toward town.

The sheriff had appeared to be a man of mixed heritage, Spanish and American. Certainly the man had spoken both English and Spanish fluently. An unimaginative man, Casey guessed, a plodding man who lived each day separately and with little thought of the future.

The jailer had been different, smiling, volatile, unreadable, the sort one might expect to find occupying a jail cell rather than guarding it.

Not long after Grinstead left, Casey heard a door slam and, going to the window, saw the sheriff striding heavily down the road toward town.

He sat down on the rough-hewn bench, worn smooth by countless previous inhabitants of the cell. He put his head down into his hands. His nerves were jumping, and his mouth tasted like cotton.

At last he got up and banged on the door. The jailer came and opened it. Behind him stood a scared, youthful guard, rifle in his hands.

Casey moved back and sat down. He said, "How about some food and water? I haven't eaten since noon."

His smoldering, frustrated anger must have been apparent, for when his eyes fell on the guard, the youth paled and backed away. The jailer only grinned. *"Sí, señor."* He turned and threw a sentence in Spanish at the boy.

The boy looked at the jailer uncertainly, but he turned and went along the corridor. The jailer lounged against the wall, smiling expectantly at Casey. "You would like to escape, *señor?*"

Casey asked sourly, "You ever have a prisoner in this hole who wouldn't?"

"Ah, but for you it is possible."

Casey looked at him suspiciously.

The guard said, "You are chasing a hundred and fifty thousand dollars that you can never catch without help from me."

Casey's interest picked up.

"I am not a greedy man, *señor.* Ten thousand would keep me in comfort for the rest of my days."

"And you think I'll give you ten thousand?"

"Why not, *señor?* If you do not, neither of us will have anything."

Casey looked at the man more closely. He wore a single gun, low on his leg, the holster tied down with rawhide. His trousers, of some black material, were tight, and he wore a greasy leather vest over a bright red shirt that was stained at the armpits with sweat.

Casey said, "You've got the wrong boy. I'm on the same side of the fence as Grinstead, only the block-headed fool won't believe it."

"*Seguro.* They all say that. 'I am innocent,' they say." Casey shrugged.

He heard the boy returning down the cor-

148

ridor. The jailer said, "I am Ramon Vigil. You will change your mind. Call me when you do."

The boy came in and set down a plate filled with highly spiced Mexican food. Then both he and the jailer backed out of the cell.

Casey ate, though he had no real appetite. Then he lay down on the bunk and closed his eyes.

Exhausted, he fell quickly into a dreamless sleep. When he woke, daylight was filtering in through the bars.

He went to the window and looked out. He saw Grinstead striding up the hill, accompanied by two of his men.

The sky was overcast, and already rain was beginning to mist downward. The air was strong with the smell of wet manure in the public corrals, with the ever-present odor of spiced food, and of cedar wood smoke. Yet it had another smell as well, that of dampened sagebrush out on the hills, and this was a smell that made confinement a special kind of torture.

Casey heard doors opening and Grinstead pushed in with his two men. Behind them the jailer, Ramon Vigil, grinned at Casey and withdrew, closing the door.

Grinstead stood a little apart from his

men, who kept their hands near the pistols at their thighs. Grinstead said harshly, "Get up. A hundred and fifty thousand dollars is just too damned much money for a man to be squeamish. Casey, I think you know where they're going." His face went bleak. "And I'm going to find out every damned thing you do know."

Casey stood up, his eyes meeting those of Grinstead defiantly. Grinstead balled his fists. Casey flicked a glance at the two against the wall, and guessed they would not shoot. Grinstead would take no chances on Casey being killed.

Casey looked back at the stageline owner. Grinstead's shoulders hunched and he took two deliberate steps toward Casey.

Casey launched himself. His left fist sank into Grinstead's middle and it was like hitting a wall. Grinstead grunted, but did not step backward. One of his huge fists caught Casey on the side of the head and knocked him across the room to crash against the adobe wall.

He bounded back from the wall and drove his head into Grinstead's belly. This time, his weight bore the man backward, and they crashed into the wall together. Grinstead's head, striking the adobe, made a dull thump.

Casey sprang to his feet. Grinstead shook his head stupidly as he got up. His eyes were glazed as though he were only half conscious, but he moved surely enough as he came warily toward Casey.

Casey picked up the bench and threw it at Grinstead's knees. The man howled and went down. Casey jumped over his prone body and bent to grab the bench again.

He caught a sound behind him, a sibilant, whispering sound, and tried to fling himself aside. From a corner of his eye he caught a flash of movement. The barrel of a gun wielded by one of the stage owner's men came down against the back of his head and his face went down and struck the floor.

He lurched to hands and knees, head hanging. In his mouth was the taste of brass, and the room was dipping and whirling.

They expected him to get up, and stood over him waiting. He twisted his body and flung it at their knees, and felt them go down across his back.

Casey came to his feet, fighting the dizziness that tried to claim him. He staggered and fell over the bench. He got up and seized one end of it. Raising it, he flung it at the two men.

The end of the bench struck one of them on the forehead and the man fell back without a sound, blood oozing from a cut on his forehead. The other leveled his gun.

Casey jumped aside, falling, rolling to the room's corner. His head banged against the heavy slop jar and he seized it and flung it at the man.

The man fired just as the slop jar struck the gun and the bullet went wide. Grinstead rushed in, swinging a heavily booted foot at Casey. Casey seized the foot and yanked. Grinstead hit the floor with a thump. Casey got up and dived across the floor toward the gun dropped by the man he had hit with the jar.

His hand closed on it just as Grinstead's boot came down on his wrist. Without letting go of the gun, Casey forced himself up, and Grinstead's feet went out from under him.

Casey had the gun. He sat, spraddle-legged, on the stone floor. One of Grinstead's men was out cold, his forehead bleeding profusely. The other, blinded by fragments of the slop jar, stood against the wall, rubbing his eyes and spewing forth a steady stream of invective.

Grinstead wiped the palms of his hands on his pants leg and grabbed for his gun. Casey fired at the ceiling. Grinstead pushed his hands out away from his body and held them there.

Casey heard the cell door open. He got up and shoved the gun into Vigil's ribs as the man rushed through the door. "Easy now, *señor*. Step outside with me and lock the door behind you."

Vigil did so. Casey relieved him of his gun. Vigil turned and glanced at him with new respect. He said, "Let me help you, *señor*. I cannot stay here now unless I wish to occupy the cell you have just left."

Casey peered at him in the gloomy corridor. "For ten thousand? Huh uh."

"I am a reasonable man, *señor*. I would bargain with you."

Casey thought of the difficulties ahead. They would be compounded by his ignorance of Spanish. He said, "I'll give you a thousand. Grinstead can't expect to recover all that money for nothing."

Vigil's face went sad. Inside the cell, Casey could hear Grinstead bellowing, followed by a thunderous racket. Grinstead was pounding on the door with the butt of his gun. Casey grinned. He asked, "You want to be the one to unlock the door and let him out?"

Vigil shuddered.

"A thousand?"

"Sí, señor."

"Let's go, then."

He did not return Vigil's gun, but instead made the man precede him down the long corridor and out into the misting drizzle of rain. They took a roundabout route into town which avoided the main road. Casey went to the stable where he'd left the black. He bought a horse for Vigil for sixty dollars. An old Spanish saddle cost him another ten.

They rode out, but once clear of the town by two or three miles Casey reined into a small ravine and handed Vigil's gun to him.

"Let's understand each other. I'm not after this money for myself. I aim to get it and return it. And I want to catch the three that took it." He described Moya, then Bell and Wagner to Vigil. He said, "Bell was the leader, so it's sure he'll have most of the loot. But Moya's the one I want most."

Vigil was silent, so Casey went on. "You know the country. From here on they might have gone in any direction but north. What are the most likely routes they might have taken?"

Vigil shrugged. "The road to Albuquerque, perhaps the road east toward Texas."

Casey nodded. "I doubt they'd go west. That's Apache land. Try the road to Texas first."

They angled east, and discovered that Bell

154

had gone this way. They circled, and discovered that Moya had gone south toward Albuquerque. Again they circled and picked up Wagner's trail heading west.

Vigil's knowledge of Spanish was invaluable, and he found out what he wanted to know in minutes. It would have taken Casey hours to obtain the same information if he obtained it at all. The wide-scattered inhabitants of this arid land talked freely to Vigil, for he was one of them. Those Casey tried to question were suspicious and more likely to lie than not.

Now that he knew his quarry had split, Casey was forced to a decision he had long dreaded. In the end, he realized, Bell was his first responsibility. His own burning desire to get hold of Moya, consuming as it was, could not obscure that.

They camped, then, for the night, half a dozen miles east of Santa Fe, being careful to leave the road and to kill their fire as soon as supper was cooked.

Casey spread his blankets. There was no reason to be afraid of Vigil at this stage of the game. Later, perhaps, when he'd caught up with Bell things would be different. Now, Vigil was as anxious as Casey to overtake Bell.

But Bell had a three-day start. And Bell

was heading into a country so big it defied description, almost staggered the imagination. Casey wondered suddenly if he were being a fool.

Grinstead would waste no time in alerting the countryside. In a week's time, Casey would be as desperately sought for as were Bell and his two compatriots. The hunter would be hunted as implacably as the outlaws. Casey forced himself to remember the stagecoach crew falling in the street of Buffalo Wallow. Then Pelton, and Gooch, and Mrs. Gooch, and the cowboy from the Ramirez ranch. Bessie Tilton and the Indian girl . . .

The difficulties of the road ahead lessened. Casey went to sleep.

CHAPTER 13

Dawn found the pair traveling. They rode hard all day through the mountains east of Santa Fe. They avoided the road when possible, but returned to it periodically to question travelers and villagers as to whether or not Bell had passed through.

They lost his trail, and picked it up again. Gradually it became apparent that he was indeed headed for the Texas panhandle, for the vast Staked Plains.

Casey doubted that the man really intended to go into the Comanche stronghold. Bell, he figured, was simply pointing a trail; once he'd established a direction, he'd change it.

So he took nothing for granted, let no easy assumptions dominate his thinking. It cost him time, but he persisted in questioning all those he met along the way.

Mountains gave way to a gradually leveling plain, to a land of vast distance, of haze upon the horizon, occasionally of mirage.

And gradually the land became wilder. No longer did they pass the adobe dwellings of Spanish or Indian farmers. Instead they began to find the sign of nomadic Comanche and Kiowa.

Ramon Vigil became uneasy and fearful. He would have turned back, but he feared traveling alone even more than he feared going ahead.

They began to travel by night and rest by day. The risk of losing Bell's trail was more than balanced by the greater risk of being captured by a wandering party of Comanches.

Days blended into weeks. They were harried by thirst and at times by hunger because they dared not risk a shot in a land where Indian sign was everywhere. Once they lay in an arroyo and watched a caravan of Comancheros wind across the plain with their high-wheeled carretas and herds of cattle and horses.

But as the days passed, so did the miles pass beneath their feet. The trail was lost, but still Casey went grimly on. Weight melted away from his body, until his wide shoulders became racks upon which his clothing hung. His face was gaunt, his eyes sunken and angry and bleak.

At first there had been much conversation in Ramon Vigil. Now there was none. They lived and traveled together, but they had little to say to each other.

They crossed the panhandle and entered the Indian territory. And here they struck the trail of cattle pointing north.

It was early morning. The sun was just poking above the plain, and the air was clear and winy. Casey slid off his horse and stared at the wide, broad trail. "Half the cattle in Texas must have come up this trail."

"Sí, señor. But where would they go?"

"Kansas is north. Maybe they went to Kansas."

It was a puzzle Casey could not solve, this movement of cattle. So they camped, to rest their gaunt, footsore horses, and perhaps to get answers to their questions from the drovers of another herd which might pass this way.

They had not long to wait. They saw the approach of another herd in the distance as a cloud of dust rose upon the horizon.

They waited, and saw at last the straggling column of grazing, long-horned beasts, urged along by their drovers, as wild and ragged as were Casey and Vigil themselves.

Vigil said, "*Señor,* we have lost the trail of Bell. But where would a man go who crosses this trail of cattle and who had his saddle-bags filled with gold? Would he not go north, for a chance to spend some of his money in the town which must surely be at the end of this trail?"

Casey said somewhat doubtfully, "It's a chance." He thought it over slowly. It was a good chance provided Bell did not know he was being followed. If he did, then it was quite possible he would do the exact opposite and go down the trail to Texas instead.

They broke camp and rode out away from the trail, and they watched the great long-horned beasts graze past the place where they had camped. They were loosely held and loosely driven at a pace that Casey guessed would cover about twelve miles a day. A point rider headed the column, followed by cattle spread out in a great, solid V and held on each side by two swing riders. At the rear, in the dust, came the drag riders and, farther back, the pack train of supplies. Far off to one side traveled the *remuda* under three guards.

Casey said, "Keep your mouth shut about Bell. We'll hire on as drovers if we can, and I'll ask enough questions to find out whether they passed him coming north. If they didn't, we'll ride with them until they reach a town."

"*Sí, señor.* It will be good to travel in daylight and to sleep at night. It will be good to stop worrying about losing our hair."

Casey, followed by Vigil, rode toward one of the swing riders. He was a middle-aged, scrawny man with a prominent Adam's apple that bobbed as he swallowed against the dryness of the trail. Casey nodded. "Where you headed?"

The man eyed him warily. "Abilene."

"Why Abilene?"

"Railroad there."

"Who's in charge?"

"Neece." The man tossed his head. "That's him behind me."

He moved on and Casey and Vigil waited. The man who approached them was thick and grizzled, and wore a full, graying beard, well stained with tobacco. A large chew bulged in his cheek. He looked at Casey and Vigil with the same wariness displayed by the other and kept his hand noticeably close to his gun.

Casey said, "I'm Casey Day. This here's Ramon Vigil. We been ridin' this Indian country so long we'd like to get a good night's sleep. How about travelin' with you to Kansas?"

"Know cattle?"

Casey shook his head.

"Hosses?"

Casey nodded.

Neece said, "All right. We lost a couple men crossin' the Red. Ten dollars apiece you'll get, between here an' Abilene. Beans an' beef. You'll fight with us if we have to fight. Run an' I'll put a bullet in your back. Be you jayhawkers after my cattle, I'll do the same."

He nodded again, and rode on, calling back over his shoulder, "Ride over to the horse herd. Tell Palacio to come see me."

Vigil grinned and Casey returned his grin. A looseness came to his body, relief after the weeks of tension. He and Vigil had eaten nothing but meat since leaving Santa Fe, and most times they'd eaten it raw because they feared to build a fire. Beans would be good. So would coffee.

They rode to the horse herd and told the Mexican wrangler that Neece wanted to see him.

The other two were youngsters, not more than fifteen or sixteen, Casey judged. Yet the two had an almost adult competence about them, a level way of looking at a man.

They drove through the hour of nooning, and did not stop until midafternoon. The drovers ate first, then a couple of them came to relieve the wranglers so that they could eat.

Eating, Casey asked the cook, "How long has this been going on?"

The man eyed him suspiciously. "How long has what been goin' on?"

"These cattle drives."

"Couple years." The man studied Casey for a moment. "Texas needs gold — the North needs beef. There's a railhead at Abilene."

Casey said, "And when you've delivered them to Abilene, you go back for more. Is that it?"

The man shook his head. "We go back, but one drive a year is about all a man can make."

"Meet any strangers heading down the trail?" Casey dropped the question casually.

"Some. Not many."

"Then you'd remember those you met?"

"Likely."

"Met any strangers the last three-four days?"

"Couple."

Casey described Bell. "Seen that one?"

"Might. You a lawman?"

Casey shook his head. "It's a private matter."

The man relaxed. "I ain't seen him."

Casey put his dishes in the wreck pan and went back to his horse. He mounted and rode back to his work.

That night, he cleaned and oiled his gun.

The days passed, and as they did, Casey's impatience began to mount. Half a dozen times he considered leaving the drive and going north alone. But the trail boss had taken them on in good faith, and the cook had given valuable information. Casey would wait.

He began to think of Abilene, and of the time when he'd face Bell. Bell, without three guns at his back. Bell, who now would have to fight alone.

He began, too, to think of home and of Lorene. Her face hovered in his thoughts and at such times he knew a sudden, overpowering loneliness and an urgency of desire that surprised him.

Two weeks after joining the drive, Casey heard the long, lonely wail of a train whistle drift out of the distance ahead. That night, he took his pay from Neece and rode out, with Ramon Vigil at his side.

They came into Abilene in darkness. They rode past the loading pens, and the long line of cars waiting on the siding. They rode up the broad, dusty street, ablaze with light, and listened like plowmen to the barkers before the garish saloons. They witnessed a gunfight in the street, and saw a drunk buffaloed by the town marshal.

There was a pungent smell to the town, compounded of cattle and manure and the sour odor of liquor that drifted from each saloon. There was the odor of horses and of sweating men, and at times a man would get a whiff of some elusive kind of perfume.

They tied their horses before a hotel, and Casey began his rounds. At each place the question was the same. "Mr. Bell registered here?"

When the clerk would shake his head, Casey would grin knowingly. "Bell's got reasons for keepin' his name unknown." Then he would describe Bell. The clerk would shake his head and Casey would move on.

The night hours passed, and the morning

began. Gradually the noise of the town abated. Drunks slept in the street, and cowhands rode, singing or silently dejected, back to their camps on the grassland surrounding the town.

Finally, in late afternoon Casey and Vigil took a room and, after eating a huge meal, slept. Casey was up with the dawn, roaming the town, looking at each face he passed. Soon Vigil joined him.

At the stockyards, men began to load the cars. The streets began to fill.

There seemed to be a new tension in Vigil, a tension that made Casey feel uneasy. Riding toward the stock pens, Vigil suddenly said, "*Señor,* I have never seen this Bell. But there is one who fits your description of him."

The man sat on the top rail of one of the loading pens. He was talking to a man inside the pen, directing the tally of steers as they were driven into a loading corral.

It was Bell. Casey reined in his horse ten feet behind Bell and listened to the run of his talk. Bell had built for himself a front of respectability.

Bell a cattle buyer! But what better way to move the yellowbacked bills than putting them in cattle? What better way to lose himself than by posing as an honest businessman? No photographs of him graced the wanted posters. Who would connect an obviously successful cattle buyer with the ragged renegade described on the poster that Casey had seen tacked to the wall in front of the marshal's office? "Dead or alive," it had said, "$10,000 reward."

Casey recalled suddenly now that Vigil had seen the poster too. He knew he should not have let Vigil get behind him. He'd been thinking of Bell, and his habit of trusting Vigil had made him forget. But would Vigil be satisfied with the thousand dollars Casey had promised him when he could pick up half the reward by delivering the two, Casey and Bell?

Casey's spine felt cold. He was squarely between the pair. If he turned to make sure of Vigil, Bell, who was already turning, would kill him.

He heard the hammer of a revolver click behind him. Vigil could be cocking the gun to help Casey take Bell. Or Vigil could just as easily be covering Casey from behind, waiting for Casey to take or kill Bell so he could then move in on Casey alone.

But it was too late now. Casey forced his thoughts from Vigil, concentrating upon the man who now stared at him so confidently from the corral rail before him. So Bell was going to brazen it out.

Casey said harshly, "Bell, move your hands out away from your body. Then turn and slide down off the fence."

Bell looked at Casey with seemingly honest bewilderment. He asked, "Are you talking to me? If you are, you've made a mistake. My name's MacArdle."

"And you're a cattle buyer. I know. Well, swing down." Anger smoldered in Casey. Here was the man who had planned and led the Buffalo Wallow raid. Here was the man responsible for the death and misery there, the man who could have checked Moya at the homesteader's shack and in the Indian village — if he'd wanted to. Maybe he hadn't wanted to. Maybe he'd enjoyed Bessie Tilton's screams, the Arapaho girl's silent agony.

Casey's voice was low and deadly. "You son of a bitch, do I have to shoot you off that fence?"

He saw Bell's eyes narrow suddenly. He saw the man beyond Bell in the corral hurry out of the line of fire. He felt Vigil behind him.

Bell muttered, "You're making a mistake." Even as he spoke, he moved, flinging himself backward toward Casey, drawing his guns while his body was in midair.

He struck the ground on his back, the fall driving the wind from him with an explosive grunt. Casey's horse spooked away from him, dancing sideways.

Bell rolled like a cat, bringing his knees under him and supporting his upper body with his left hand. His right hand held the gun, which was rising, hammer already thumbed back.

Casey fired, and the bullet took Bell's left arm out from under him and dumped him back in the dirt. Lying on his left side, he raised his gun again.

Casey fought his plunging, rearing mount, trying to line his gun. Bell fired, and the bullet whistled over Casey's head.

Now Bell took time to rise, pulling himself up by the poles of the corral fence, as Casey fought his mount. Upright, he raised his gun deliberately, aiming. His face was gray with pain.

Desperate, Casey snapped a shot. This bullet caught Bell in the chest and drove him back against the fence. The poles rattled with the impact. Somehow Bell found the strength to raise his arm again, and again he looked at Casey along the barrel of the gun.

Casey's iron hand on his horse's reins stopped the horse — momentarily only, but long enough. His bullet hit Bell in the throat, and the man's gun muzzle dropped. He slid down the fence, blood streaming from the severed jugular vein in his throat.

Casey swung his head, now trying to turn his horse. Before he could complete the turn, a gun blasted behind him and a bullet seared along the hard, tight muscles of his thigh. Inside the corral a man yipped with sudden pain as the bullet struck him.

Again Vigil's gun roared, its concussion now deafening Casey's ears. The bullet missed. Casey's horse reared and pawed the air. Casey brought him down with a blow of the gun muzzle between his ears. Stunned, the horse was still.

Casey saw Vigil's widened eyes as the man fired wildly at him, the tense set of Vigil's mouth. Fear had replaced greed and avarice in those dark eyes. As Casey swung his gun, Vigil flinched against the expected impact of Casey's bullet.

But something held Casey back, a reluctance to kill this man who had been his companion so many weeks. His spurs sank into his horse's sides and the horse leaped ahead, turning sideways against the cutting rake of Casey's right spur.

The horse collided with Vigil's mount. Casey rammed the barrel of his gun savagely into Vigil's belly, and as the man doubled toward him, brought it down against the back of Vigil's head.

Vigil's horse leaped away, and Vigil slid headfirst out of the saddle, hit the ground and lay quite still.

Casey swung around. The loaders watched him silently, mouths agape. The one who had been shot sat on the ground, staring stupidly first at the bloodsoaked leg of his pants, then up at Casey, whose gun still smoked in his hand.

Casey said sharply, "MacArdle, here — where was he staying?"

"Drover's Hotel." The answer came quickly, breathlessly, from two men at once.

"Did he pay for the cattle he bought by cash or draft?"

"Hadn't paid yet, mister. He promised to pay in cash."

Casey said, "Get your man and Vigil here to a doctor."

He swung his horse and set the spurs. The animal leaped ahead, confused, but more than ready to run. Casey headed toward the Drover's Hotel, which was in the center of town.

CHAPTER 14

Riding, Casey tried to calculate how long it would be before the hue and cry began. Long enough, he hoped, for him to do what he intended doing.

Shock would immobilize those at the loading pen for a while. One of them would run for the doctor, and that would take time.

He yanked his horse in before the Drover's Hotel. He took the steps at a bound, but slowed as he crossed the threshold and entered the large, cool lobby.

To the clerk he said urgently, "MacArdle. I've got to see him quick. Which room?"

"Two fourteen. But Mr. MacArdle has gone . . ."

Casey was already halfway up the stairs. He ran along the carpeted hall, glancing frequently at room numbers.

Two fourteen was locked. Casey stood back and kicked at the lock. The door burst open and Casey went in.

His glance raced around the room. There was a slight bulge in the thin mattress and he yanked it off the bed. There on the springs lay Bell's saddlebags, bulging and full.

Casey's spirits lifted, but he had to make sure; he opened both saddlebags and inspected the bundles of yellowbacked bills inside. He closed them, swung them over his shoulder and went out.

He rushed down the stairs past the pop-eyed stuttering clerk, who had both heard the door crash and seen the saddlebags. In the street, Casey saw a kid running toward the marshal's office, glancing frequently and with obvious fright over his shoulder.

He heard the uproar down by the loading pens as he mounted his horse. Reining around, he saw the marshal coming toward the shouting boy, gun in hand. The boy turned and pointed at Casey.

Casey spurred his horse and raced out of town. A few people turned to stare as he galloped past, but nobody made a move to stop him.

He cleared the town and was out on the grass. He turned west immediately, slowing his horse to a mile-eating lope.

Suddenly it was very quiet around him. The only sound in his ears was the wind rustling the long grass and the pounding beat of his horse's hoofs. Occasionally, in the distance, he could hear the deep bellow of a bull.

He wondered how much of a jump he had. Maybe half an hour. It should take that long for the marshal to listen to the stories of the witnesses and gather men for a posse.

For the first time in weeks, he felt easy. He had a good horse under him. He had the lion's share of the stagecoach loot. Bell was dead; a part of the job was done.

It lifted him up. He'd followed Bell across a thousand miles of empty, hostile land, and he'd found him. All the difficulties of tracing Wagner and Moya seemed suddenly less than they had before.

He permitted himself to think of Lorene. He even considered swinging past Buffalo Wallow before going west to the mountains. But then he thought of Vigil, who would tell the story of the captured loot held by a man whose picture was on posters from one end of the country to the other. The news would go out over the wires, would reach Buffalo Wallow days before Casey could.

It wouldn't do. He shook his head and rode on.

From here on, it was avoid all towns, avoid all contact with other people; lose himself in the plain's vastness, so that if they trailed him they'd have to trail by guess, as he had been forced to do with Bell.

On a rise of land five miles west of town, he swung his horse and looked behind. The land lay there like a rolling sea of grass. Beyond the town he could see the dark masses which were the herds grazing, awaiting their turns at the cars.

He saw a buggy moving along a road, a dot in the distance. And he found what his eyes sought too, a group of horsemen moving out from the edge of town, coming toward him, raising a dust cloud that told Casey the speed at which they were traveling.

He turned and moved on, loping a while, then trotting, then walking. Every hour he halted for what he judged to be five minutes, off-saddled, and rubbed his horse's steaming sides with the saddle blanket.

The posse gained, but only slightly, for offsetting the time Casey spent caring for his horse was the time the posse lost in following his trail.

The sun rose to its zenith; it was blazing hot at midday. Casey had no food with him but he was not hungry — yet. He tried to utilize the contours of the land so as to avoid being seen, but the rolling plain afforded little cover. In midafternoon, a distant shot behind him signaled that he had failed. They had sighted him; they would press on toward the spot where one of them had sighted him.

He glanced at the sky, gauging the amount of daylight left. If he could stay ahead until dark, he could change his course, and then change it again; he'd leave them farther and farther behind as the night progressed.

Tomorrow, though, the posse would no doubt commandeer fresh horses somewhere along the way. That was a risk that had to be taken. Tonight, however, the advantage would be his.

The sun dropped behind the plain's western rim. Briefly it stained the clouds a brilliant orange. Then all was gray, a gray that deepened slowly to dusk and finally to full darkness.

Casey figured the posse had closed the distance between them to three miles. It was a slim margin at best. But perhaps enough.

He considered what they would expect of him now that dark had come. He decided they'd be watching for him to branch away from his present course. So he deliberately stayed upon it, traveling this way for a full three hours.

Once in the distance behind him he saw the winking of a lantern by which they followed his trail. It moved almost imperceptibly. For the first time, Casey smiled. The advantage was truly his.

He changed course, riding south. He struck a broad, sandy stream bed, and rode in the trickle of water for a couple of hours.

Then he emerged and headed south again.

He passed farms and ranches, and avoided their dark buildings. But as dawn streaked the sky with gray, he sought one out, one whose grassy pasture held a ban of loose horses.

He roped out a dun-colored mare that appeared to be the best of the lot and transferred his saddle to her. Trailing his own riderless mount, he rode away.

The posse would eventually find this place, he knew, then horse stealing would be added to the crime of which he was already accused. He intended to turn the dun mare loose when the black had had a chance to rest.

At almost a mile, he heard a rifle back at the rancher's house. The bullets came nowhere near, though he heard one ricochet. He cursed softly under his breath; he'd hoped he'd be long gone before the mare's owner awoke.

He traveled another ten miles before he saw the rancher trailing him, alone, almost a mile back.

Casey dismounted and flung himself prone. He placed three rifle bullets within thirty feet of the galloping rancher. He saw the man stop, and turn away, heading for a neighbor or a nearby town, Casey guessed.

He remounted and went on.

After that, the day passed uneventfully, and he slept that night for four hours. When he awoke, he released the mare and rode on mounted upon the black, which seemed rested again.

Days passed, and he saw neither the posse from Abilene nor the rancher behind him. He assumed the rancher had come upon his mare and had returned with her, satisfied to have her back.

Perhaps the posse had given up, but even if they had it didn't make Casey's position any more secure. They simply assigned the task of capturing him to other law-enforcement officers in the towns ahead.

Days grew into weeks. Living off the country, Casey crossed the Kansas line and came again into Colorado.

Another week passed, during which Casey traveled but a few miles a day while he rested his horse and himself, while he hunted and gorged himself on the meat. There was restlessness in him and a strong sense of urgency, but he curbed these feelings determinedly. He had been on the trail a long, long time. A few days for resting would be well spent.

He went to considerable pains avoiding the traveled routes, traveling cross-country.

He avoided occasional homestead shacks he passed, going out of his way to detour around them. He avoided Indians with a skill born of practice gained during the past months.

And at last, one morning he saw the snowy peaks of the mountains ahead.

Sight of them should have lifted his spirits; but it did not. He had been too long alone; he was grown bitter. The anger that simmered in his heart against the outlaws had festered and grown until he felt a pervading enmity toward all mankind. Too many men's hands were against him, and they had been against him for too long a time. Grinstead, who should have helped him, lumped him with the outlaws and hunted him as relentlessly as Casey did the remaining two. Vigil had betrayed him.

Casey's face had grown into a mask of implacable hardness; his eyes had turned into bits of stone. His beard, red-brown, was a ragged two inches long. His hair had grown until it covered his neck and all but hid his ears. His clothes were stiff with sweat and dust.

The weight he had lost during the journey across Texas had come back to his gaunt frame, but now it was all tough sinew and muscle.

As Casey hardened, so did the black gelding. Without shoes for weeks, the black now grew sore-footed, for his hoofs grew as fast as they wore away.

It would be different in the mountains, traveling forever across sharp-edged rock. So Casey rode into a town, a place called Pueblo, and turned the horse over to a smith to be shod.

He stopped before the jail to stare at his picture on a wanted poster glued to the fly-specked window. He scratched his beard, fingered his long hair. He hadn't thought of them as a disguise, but now he realized with pleased satisfaction that they were. He bought ammunition in a store, and a sack of groceries, coffee, salt and dried beans. Going back, he stopped and stared again at the wanted poster.

A pair of passing men stopped, and stared, then studied the poster after Casey had hurried on. Glancing back, he saw one of them drawing a beard on his picture with a pencil stub that he moistened frequently in his mouth.

The shoeing was finished. Casey inspected the job and paid the blacksmith's charge. Mounting, he rode west and north until he struck the Arkansas River.

Wagner had gone west from Santa Fe. Casey tried to remember the few maps he'd seen of the country. He knew Wagner could have gone on to California. He might also have lighted for good somewhere in Arizona. He might have turned north once he got west of the mountains. He might be in Utah, or in western Colorado. He might even be in Wyoming.

Casey tried to remember Wagner, tried to recall the man's face. He failed. All he could remember were Wagner's eyes. The greed that had been in them. The avarice . . .

A greedy man was never satisfied with what he had. So Wagner would not be satisfied. He would want more, and more. There would likely be no end to his acquisitiveness. . . . Where would a greedy man, one who had a big stake, go?

Casey considered that all evening without result. Finally he killed his fire and wrapped himself in blankets against the growing chill in the air. His mind stayed with the problem; what area might attract a man like Wagner in his circumstances?

So far as Casey knew, there were no places in Arizona where a man could get rich quick. The gold rush was over in California; the Argonauts had scattered. . . .

Casey's pulse began to stir with excitement. Fortunes were coming out of the

Colorado mountains. Mining towns were scattered through them.

What better place for a man with a stake to go? He could double his stake, already a fortune, by buying claims, or running a saloon, or freighting in supplies.

Casey decided he would snoop around. He'd look in on a few of these bonanza towns. If he failed to find Wagner, then he could always go on to Arizona and California.

He went to sleep quickly.

He didn't know exactly what it was that woke him. But his trail-sharpened nerves were tight, his ears attuned to the night sounds around him. There was something . . . not right, something that had impaired the night's muted symphony.

In the gorge, the Arkansas tumbled onward with a steady roar. Far off, a coyote yipped his lonely cry. The cold night wind sighed through the long-leafed ponderosa pines. A branch cracked. . . .

Instantly Casey's hand closed upon his gun. Carefully, slowly, he eased out of his blankets. He picked up the saddlebags, upon which his head had been pillowed.

He still wore his pants, but he had taken off his shirt and boots. The toes of his socks were gone, and the pine needles underfoot stung his feet and collected inside the worn socks.

Silently as a Cheyenne brave, he traveled along for twenty yards or so, then stopped beside the thick trunk of a huge tree. Another twig snapped; Casey's horse whinnied eagerly. Casey flung two shots toward his camp, and stepped behind the trunk of the tree.

A man cried out in brief, pungent profanity. Casey stuck his head around the tree trunk and triggered two more shots. This time answering shots chunked into the tree trunk, scattering bark to right and left.

Casey yelled boldly, "Make tracks, you dry-gulching bastards! You got ten seconds, and then I'm comin' for you!"

He heard them talking in low voices — two, he judged. He began to circle silently. He reached his horse so quietly the animal started when he touched its neck. But it smelled him, and quieted.

Casey hung the saddlebags in the heavy branches of a nearby pine. Then he fashioned a hackamore from the picket rope, cut off the excess with his knife.

He mounted bareback. The horse tensed under him. Suddenly Casey's knees gripped, and his heels drummed on the horse's ribs.

The black surged toward the camp. Casey

fired past his neck, directly at the camp, then loosed a shrill Arapaho war cry.

He thundered through the camp. He felt the shock as the black bowled one man over and sent him spinning into underbrush. He yanked back on the hackamore, aware that his upper body, clad in a once-white suit of long underwear, presented the only target available.

But the brazen horseback charge had undermined the spirit of the attackers. He heard them scurrying down the hill, then, a moment later, their horses scrambling downward over the rocky ground, starting slides as they took the steep trail.

They were the two, no doubt, who had spotted his resemblance to the picture on the wanted poster. And they'd be back, or others would, for another crack at the man who carried a fortune with him, who was worth another delivered in Denver City.

Casey packed up in darkness and rode on. He knew a stark aloneness, knew the feel of a hunted wolf, knew the fierceness that comes when every other living thing seems to want death for the hunted.

A bitter man, an angry and dangerous man, Casey realized at last the size and the meaning of the task he had set for himself, what he had gambled when he did. Success, if it came, would put him in the clear with Grinstead, would give him peace of mind within himself.

But what if he killed in the course of this long pursuit? What if a lawman died, or another, whose only crime was greed, whose only desire was to help capture a man proclaimed an outlaw from one end of the land to the other?

For the first time Casey began to feel afraid. It was not fear for his own life, but for the lives of the men who might still try to stop him.

He thought of Buffalo Wallow and of Lorene. He faced the likelihood that before he was through he would truly become an outlaw, morally as well as legally, because of acts he might commit during the course of his self-ordained pursuit.

Then he thought of Moya, and of Wagner. He deliberately put the idea of giving up away from him. Afterward he clung desperately to the hatred that had sustained him thus far. It would continue to sustain him only if he did not let it slip away, if he nourished and fed it with the fuel of an undiluted, unreasoning dedication.

CHAPTER 15

A succession of gold camps passed before him, live towns and dead ones, booming ones and fading ones. Autumn came, and the leaves in the high country turned gold and fell off onto ground that was white with snow.

Once he was caught by a blizzard in a high mountain pass; the dark angel hovered close, but Casey's number was not up. Afterward he came slowly down into a new town called Oro City. Leading his sore-footed black, he limped along California Gulch, the valley that cradled the town.

A typical gold town, Oro City sprawled on both sides of the valley. Placer diggings dotted the stream that meandered through it. The hillsides were pocked with prospect holes. Farther down the gulch was a tent city, and there were a few cabins, built of logs and chinked with mud, roofed with poles and brush over which a thick layer of dirt had been thrown. From some of these grew a profusion of dying weeds.

Casey paid five dollars to stable his horse, then peeled off another five for a cot in one of the tents. He carried the money now in a bulging money belt strapped around his middle. It was painfully uncomfortable, but it would be harder to steal than a pair of loose saddlebags.

He crawled into the filthy blankets without removing his clothes. It made no difference to Casey that he himself was dirty, his clothes and his body stinking with sweat. Gradualy he began to thaw out.

He slept, and awoke, and after a shorter sleep, rose to prowl the town in night's first bitter chill. One street of the "city" was lined wholly with saloon tents, and Casey began his rounds. He bought a drink in each, but he drank the raw whisky only in the first two places he visited.

His beard, so long that it was beginning to curl, hid his face except for his cheeks and his nose. His battered hat, worn low on his forehead, concealed the implacable coldness of his eyes, but every once and again a man, peering at him curiously in the dim light, would catch their menacing gleam and quickly look away.

Women came to him, smiling their false, tired smiles, and went away, smiles fading as Casey put his glance upon them; some of these could not repress the shiver of uneasy fear that ran through them as they turned aside.

The last of the long line of saloons, larger than the others, was also more brightly lighted. The women here looked less jaded, and there was even a low stage at one end of the tent, and a tinkling, off-key piano.

Casey looked about quickly, hopefully, but he saw no man that he knew, certainly nobody large enough to be the one he sought. Discouragement, bleak and bitter, hit him. The shadow of hope that had touched him when he first saw Oro City faded and died. He was discouraged, brutally tired. It was hopeless, hopeless. . . . He shook himself; he would not give up! Wagner might be in some other business. Perhaps in this very camp. It was time to start asking a few questions. . . .

Casey downed two more drinks in quick succession. The whisky lay warm in his stomach. An alcoholic well-being lightened his thoughts. His eyes softened and he felt the tight, hard muscles of his face relax a little.

A girl came toward him, smiling hesitantly. This time Casey returned the smile. This one looked like a real woman, not like a tired, used-up strumpet. . . .

She came up beside him and put a hand on his arm. Her voice was low, her words softly welcoming. "Lonesome? Want to dance?" She looked at him, pity in her eyes. "Or would you rather just talk?"

She was a small-statured girl in her early twenties. What she was showed in her eyes, but she had not yet developed the hardness that was stamped so indelibly on the faces of the others.

Casey smiled at her again. He realized suddenly, poignantly, how long it had been since he had responded to another person's friendly approach. "Talk . . ." he said. "Yes, talk. Is there a table?"

"Sure. Come on." She nodded at the bartender and he slid two drinks onto the bar. Casey paid for them, then carried the filled glasses after the girl.

She had located a vacant place in a far corner of the tent. Casey put the drinks on the table and sat down. He looked at the girl and surprised her appraising glance upon him.

She asked, "You a miner, mister? I haven't seen you here before."

Casey shook his head. "I just got here today. I'm looking for a man who might be here. Maybe you've seen him." He described Wagner swiftly.

As he talked, something within the girl withdrew. Her eyes narrowed slightly, and her mouth tightened almost imperceptibly.

"You know him?" Casey's question was almost a triumphant statement.

She shook her head but it could not convince him. Casey said quietly, "I could tell you some of the things he's done. I could tell you I wasn't a lawman. But I don't suppose it would make any difference." He paused, then said, "He's either here or he has been here — which is it?"

She studied him carefully. "I wonder if you realize what hunting this man has done to you." She looked at him in pity and wonder.

"I don't care about that." He watched her eagerly, hopefully, and waited. . . .

This girl reminded him of Lorene. Casey tossed off his drink. The warmth of it coursed down his throat and spread through all of him. He leaned against the back of the chair. Over the odors of whisky and man-sweat, her perfume drifted to him. He eyed her soft skin, her warm eyes; for the first time in months woman hunger stirred within him. It didn't seem to matter that she would not respond to his question.

"What we need is a couple more drinks." Recklessness was rising in Casey; the watchfulness that had become so much a part of him was lost, at least for a while. She nodded, unspeaking, and he got up and walked to the bar. The money in his pocket was not enough; he reached inside his shirt, into the money belt, and brought out a crisp twenty.

He walked back to the table, the bottle in his hand. He poured the girl a drink and looked at her for a long moment. "What's your name?" he asked.

"Ruby."

"All right, Ruby," he said. "Drink up, girl; then I've got to go. If you won't tell me what I want to know, I'll find someone else who will."

"I'll tell you," she said. "On one condition."

"Name it," he said, watching her face.

"That you'll — forget him for tonight."

Casey looked at her. She reminded him very much of Lorene, he told himself. He felt the hunger more keenly; the recklessness mounted.

"All right," he said.

"He was here, but he's gone," she told him. "He used to own this joint."

Casey sat up straight. "How long has he been gone?"

"What difference does that make?" she said to him. "What difference, tonight?"

"You know where he went?" he shot at her.

She shook her head, and bitterness touched her face briefly.

Casey said, "Were you in love with him?"

She shook her head again, wearily this time. "You promised you'd forget him for tonight," she reminded him.

Casey could not quiet the pounding blood in his body. He looked steadily at the girl and she met his glance with a direct one of her own. Tonight wouldn't matter. He couldn't go chasing after Wagner in the dark.

He said, "You have a tent of your own?"

Her eyes held his. "A cabin."

He picked up the bottle. "Come on," he said huskily.

For a moment her eyes seemed to hold doubt, but then she got up and preceded him silently into the cold, dark, rutted street.

She led the way up the hillside to a small, one-room cabin. She went in and lighted a lamp. Casey built up the fire in the stove. When it was roaring steadily, he turned to her. The doubt was back in her eyes for a moment, but she came to him, putting her hands on his shoulders, offering her lips.

He kissed her long and hard. His blood was afire; his whole being ached with a need so intense that he could scarcely move. Finally, when he did, he was so clumsy and awkward that she laughed gently as she undid her own clothing and turned down the lamp.

He was direct and eager then, but there

was a gentleness about him and a consideration that surprised the girl and touched her.

Afterward, as they lay quietly, she looked steadily at him, and tears misted her dark eyes. She murmured, "I wondered about you. . . . Now I know."

"Know what?"

"You aren't hard and cruel — the way you look on the outside. Casey, give it up. Stay here in Oro City. Stake a claim. . . ."

His eyes grew cold again and he shook his head. He got up and poured himself another drink from the bottle.

The girl rose, slipped into a wrapper and said quietly, "I'll make some coffee."

For a while she busied herself at the stove. The strong, pleasant aroma of coffee filled the cabin. Casey sat beside the stove and talked. He told her about Buffalo Wallow and the four men who had come to rob the stage. He told her of the people killed and wounded, of Bessie Tilton and the Arapaho girl.

When he had finished, he said, "You see why I won't give up? Why I can't give up?"

"Yes," she said, without looking at him. "I see."

"Tell me about Wagner now."

"He left earlier tonight. He saw you in the

street this afternoon. I didn't know it was you then, but another girl and I heard some talk about it. I never saw a man more scared. He sold his saloon within ten minutes after he saw you. Then he pulled out. He's trying to make it over the pass before it gets snowed in for the winter."

Casey came to his feet. He took several yellowbacks from the money belt and laid them on the rickety table. She opened her mouth to beg him to stay, but after a look at his eyes she closed it again without speaking.

He put his hand on the door. "You've been good for me," he said to her.

She shook her head, her eyes bright, and this time she said it: "Casey, stay here."

He went out quickly and closed the door behind him. He walked down the hill to the town and found the stable where he'd left his horse. A few bearded men wandered in the streets, an unending traffic from saloon to saloon. Noise rolled tumultuously from the tents into the streets.

Casey hated to give up the black, which had served him faithfully and well, but he had no choice. The horse was too sore-footed to travel.

The stableman, a gray-bearded oldster with a nose like a sharp-pointed stick and eyes as shrewd as a pawnbroker's, showed Casey half a dozen horses he had for sale. In lantern light, Casey inspected them carefully.

None was as strong as the black but there was a big sorrel gelding, short-coupled and long of leg. He was hammer-headed and wicked-eyed, but Casey thought he'd do. Paying a hundred dollars' boot on the trade, Casey saddled and rode up the street.

At the edge of town he found a restaurant which offered food soup-kitchen style; the customer ate squatting on the ground in front of the tent. Casey bought a plate of stew and a mug of coffee and wolfed it down. A cold wind knifed down off the pass, chilling him to the bone in spite of the hot food and his heavy mackinaw. It began to snow, tiny flakes that would grow in size as the storm progressed. Yet not even the prospect of a night's travel in a blinding snowstorm could dull the edge of exultation that leaped within Casey Day.

He had his plate refilled with stew, and this time he ate more slowly. There was no telling when he'd have another hot meal. From the heavy-set, middle-aged woman who ran the place he bought a sack of beans, a piece of salt pork, and a small sack of coffee. These he tied behind his saddle.

Then he mounted and rode out in the direction of the pass, moving through the town with caution, his hand never far from his gun. He knew how it was in these gold towns at night. A lot of money changed hands, not all of it inside the saloons and the gambling halls.

A couple of shots racketed off to his right, and a man's high yell of pain punctuated them. Someone else began to curse loudly, a stream of obscene invective that went on steadily until Casey rode out of earshot.

A moment or so later he heard a woman scream. A dog began to bark. A man staggered past him and collapsed in the snow, breathing heavily. Fine place for him to sleep off his drink, Casey thought sardonically.

The flakes of snow were larger now. A shadow moved out from the black lee of a tent and fell in behind Casey, slipping along like a ghost. Snow drove into Casey's face, blinding him.

He heard a sound behind him. He whirled in the saddle, grabbing for his gun.

Hands seized his leg and yanked him from the saddle. He hit hard, frozen ground with a thump.

They were on him then, three or four of them, Casey couldn't tell how many. He

195

fought with single-minded ferocity, a belea-
guered animal fighting for its life. His gun
blasted, and one of them fell away. The
slashing gun barrel put another down limp
in the snow before the weapon was somehow knocked from his hand.

He was up, then, moving away. They
rushed him, the two that were left, coming
out of the blinding snow like shadows. Casey leaped aside. His foot came down on
the point of a miner's pick, standing beside
a tent and the handle flew up to whack his
knee.

For an instant pain made the world swim
before his eyes. Then he grabbed the handle
and swung the pick in a wide arc. He let it
go; it twisted through the darkness and took
the legs out from under one of the men
rushing at him.

The man shouted hoarsely as he went
down, writhing, in the snow; the other fell
over him, then struggled to his feet and fled.

Casey hurdled the down man and
searched around in the snow for his gun.
He found it, snatched it up, holstered it,
and turned back to his horse.

He had thought it was over, but now the
man who had fled came back, came rushing
at him from behind a tent, swinging a two-
by-four in both hands.

The vicious blow struck Casey on the back and drove him against his horse. The animal spooked away and Casey collapsed in the snow.

The man swung the club again, and this time hit the side of Casey's head a glancing blow.

Half-conscious, he felt hands fumbling at his money belt. Damn his own stupidity, he thought dully. He should never have taken money from the belt back there in the saloon.

His hand moved uncertainly toward his holstered gun. He got it out, rammed it against the body bending above him, thumbed back the hammer and pulled the trigger. There was a muffled explosion and the man grunted, straightened up, and fell over backward.

Casey got up, took a step, staggered and fell. He struggled to his feet a second time and peered around, searching for his horse. His head was reeling; he was dizzy and sick.

Finally he saw the horse and stumbled toward it. It moved away, frightened. He pursued it at a shambling run, cursing it savagely.

He was soaked with sweat and melted snow and when he stopped, panting, he shook with a sudden chill. But suddenly the horse stopped. Casey reached it and found someone holding it.

He muttered, "Thanks for catching him. I . . ."

He fell against the horse. He heard a voice. "Casey, you can't travel tonight. You're hurt."

It was Ruby. There was compassion in her voice, and worry.

He muttered, "I've got to go."

"Will it help any to die up there in that pass? Rest tonight, Casey. Go on tomorrow."

He tried to pull away. Weakness came over him like a drifting fog. At last he said wearily, "All right . . . all right, Ruby. Get me — into a bed. . . ."

She helped him up the hill to her cabin and stabled his horse behind it. She put a compress of snow on his injured head. She rubbed the bruised muscles of his back with liniment. At last he fell into a sound sleep and she looked at his face.

The features were no longer grim. She smiled a small, tired smile.

Chapter 16

He woke at dawn. The half-light was gray and chill. The fire in the stove had gone out and it was achingly cold. He could see his breath in the air inside the cabin.

Ruby was snuggled warmly against him. For a few moments he looked at her face, relaxed in sleep and softly pretty. Pity for her touched him, anger at the way life had treated her. He wished she didn't have to live the way she must. She would stay on here, though, until time stole her prettiness and what gentleness was left in her.

He got up. Trying not to waken her, he built up the fire and put on water for coffee. A nervous restlessness stirred him, a driving compulsion to be gone.

He looked outside and saw that the night had left about eight inches of snow on the ground. Up on the pass it was probably more, enough to make the going hard. But not enough to keep him from going through . . .

The cabin warmed, and Ruby awakened. She smiled at him sleepily. He went over to the bunk and kissed her. She giggled as his beard tickled her throat.

Then she sobered. "Do you have to go this morning? Can't you stay?"

"I can't do it, Ruby. I've damned near a year of my life tied up in this. I've got to go on, while either Wagner or Moya stays alive."

She studied him carefully. The life ebbed

from her face. "I suppose you do. It was foolish, what I was think . . . hoping."

He said, "You're young and pretty, Ruby. There's a man for you somewhere."

For a while she was silent. Then she got up and began to put her clothes on.

"Casey," she said, "I'll try to do something about myself if you'll do the same."

He looked at her questioningly.

"You've got to take the first step that will put you in the clear with the law. Why don't you turn in the money you're carrying?"

He frowned. "Now how could I do that?"

"Don't you know someone in Buffalo Wallow — someone you can trust?"

He thought about Lorene Mowrey and nodded.

"A girl?"

Again he nodded.

"Then take the money to her. Have her turn it over to the authorities after you're safely away. It will take the pressure off you, Casey. And you won't have to run the risk of being robbed of it."

He considered the idea. There was good sense in it. The money was one of the things about which he worried the most. And it *would* serve to take some of the pressure off him.

"I'll do it," he told her. He shrugged into

his coat.

She came to him and put her arms around him with a suggestion of desperation. "Good luck, Casey Day," she said, and kissed him on the lips.

He went out and saddled his horse and rode around in front of the cabin. She was standing in the doorway and she looked even younger and prettier than she had looked last night. Casey fought down a lump in his throat. She waved to him, and Casey returned her wave before he rode down the slope. He went through the waking town, heading east toward the pass he had crossed to reach this place.

As he rode, clouds began to form over the high peaks. They spread swiftly and within an hour they blotted out the sun. Within two hours it had begun to snow again, big, heavy flakes that would pile five or six inches an hour upon the already thickly covered ground.

Uneasiness stirred in Casey. At this rate, the pass might well be closed before he reached it. He knew how risky it was to set out alone in the dead of winter to travel the high country, but that knowledge was as nothing compared to the power that drove him on. If he failed to get across the pass now, he wouldn't get another chance until spring.

He climbed steadily all morning toward the bare, white peaks where snow drifted on a hurricane wind, blinding, stinging, piling up giant drifts, drifts that could swallow a man and his horse and not leave a trace. . . .

The horse fought for his head, but Casey clung grimly to the reins with a numbing hand and, with brutal spurs, forced the animal on.

He lost the road, found it, lost it again. His horse floundered into a gully and fell. Casey kept an iron clutch on the reins and mounted again as the horse scrambled to his feet.

When the cold became too intense to endure, he reined into a thick patch of timber. Sheltered from the knifelike wind, he flailed his arms until circulation was restored and stamped his feet until the blood came back to them, bringing excruciating pain in its wake.

He went on, a dark figure, buffeted by the wind whose awful intensity increased with the passing of each blind, brutal hour.

He judged he was near the top of the pass now, near the tiny cabin that had saved his life the day before yesterday, when he had narrowly missed freezing to death.

Suddenly he thought he heard a sound ahead of him. He stopped and waited. He heard nothing more.

He went on until, through the shroud of snow ahead, he saw the dim outline of the cabin.

Some primeval caution touched him with uneasiness. He halted. The bark of a rifle came flat and dead, and was snatched away by the howling wind.

His horse shied, and Casey dug his spurs unhesitatingly into the animal's sides. He could not go back; he was not going back. He couldn't detour around the cabin; on each side of the road were drifts that could trap and bury him. He thundered upward toward the cabin which materialized abruptly out of the snow, becoming plain and clearly defined as he drew abreast of it.

Two men stood before it, and the size of one of them was unmistakable: Wagner! Each had a rifle at his shoulder, sighting along the barrel.

Crouched low over the withers of the running horse, Casey thought grimly that now the hunted had turned hunter. Wagner had waited here to ambush him, counting on Casey's returning this way before the pass was closed.

The cabin was behind him. Casey heard

the angry buzz of a bullet close to his head. Then he was swallowed into the blinding clouds of drifting snow.

He hauled the horse to a halt, uncertain for a moment what he should do now. Should he go on? Or should he lay an ambush of his own?

He saw he had to go on. Neither he nor the horse could stand much more of this bitter cold. It would be a poor bargain for him to kill Wagner and then die himself of the cold. . . .

He urged the horse ahead. He knew that Wagner would come on behind him as swiftly as he could. Later, at some lower elevation, perhaps he could waylay the man.

The rest of the day was an eternity of screeching wind, of savage cold. But as the road dropped, the storm abated and, an hour after dark, Casey stumbled into a deserted miner's cabin and collapsed upon the floor.

Figuring that Wagner would be traveling more slowly, fearful of being ambushed in turn, Casey slept in complete exhaustion for almost an hour. Then, after a quick scout outside, he built a fire and cooked himself a meal. When he had eaten, he found a sack of grain hanging from a rafter where it was safe from mice and gave his horse a feed.

In darkness, then, he went on. He put his horse into the swift-flowing stream by the road at once, and did not leave it until he came to a windswept, rocky place where he could leave without making a trail. After that, he backtracked, staying high on the hillside until he came to the cabin again.

He dismounted, tied his horse, and huddled in the lee of a rock to watch. He had scarcely taken up his position when he saw the sparks of a newly-kindled fire shoot from the chimney.

He spent the night waiting there, alternately huddling and stamping his feet and flailing his arms. When Wagner and his companion departed at dawn, he set out in pursuit. He smiled grimly to himself when he saw them pass the place where he had come out of the stream. Wagner was again the hunted; he did not realize that Casey Day was now behind him.

And yet, as he followed, Casey became gradually aware that Wagner was traveling, not as a man following a trail, but as one who knows his destination. He speculated on the meaning of this. The three bandits very probably had worked out some system of getting in touch with each other. Perhaps they had settled upon a town where they could send letters to each other, and had taken other names so that the letters would not be noticed.

It would be easy enough to address a letter to someone in care of General Delivery and mark it "please hold." Easy enough for a man passing through to stop at the post office and ask if any mail was being held for him. Or to write there and ask that such mail be forwarded to him.

In this way, they could have been communicating with each other all along. Thus, Wagner might have learned Moya's whereabouts; if he was as scared as Ruby had thought him to be, he might be planning to join forces with Moya again.

Conscious of the increasing evidence of haste in Wagner's trail, Casey spurred his horse ahead. Wagner and his companion were crowding their horses almost beyond endurance.

Wagner *must* be getting scared. By this time, having found no sign of Casey's being ahead of him, he must be acting on the assumption that Casey was behind. *If* he knew where Moya was, he'd be heading there as quickly as possible; Moya's gun would count a lot when Casey finally caught up....

The horse jumped from the involuntary jab of Casey's spurs — and faltered. With a silent curse, Casey drew him in and let him walk. Damn it, if he only had the black under him!

He came down out of the mountains, losing Wagner's trail where the snow had thawed, finding it again where there was mud or where the ground was soft. And at last, out on the plain where the grass was thick and where there was no snow, he lost it for good.

His horse played out with his frantic effort to find it again. He found a stagecoach way station and paid fifty dollars to trade horses.

Reluctantly, he remembered his promise to Ruby. Well, the trail was lost. He could keep his promise with a loss of no more than a couple of days. With it kept, he could return and pick up Wagner's trail. Maybe now it would lead him to Moya too. . . .

Half exhausted, turned wild by months of hunting and being hunted, Casey began to think more and more of Moya. He dwelt lovingly on the idea of killing Moya, slowly, torturingly. But the sun was bright, the air like wine, and suddenly Casey shuddered. Self-disgust overwhelmed him. He had hated so long that he was becoming a twisted thing, almost inhuman. Maybe it would be a good idea to forget the hunt a while, he thought. Good to see Lorene again . . .

Holding his horse to a steady lope, Casey watched sweat build up on the animal's neck as he rode toward Buffalo Wallow. He smelled the steamy, rank odor that rose from the horse's flanks. The day passed, and the sun dropped behind the mountains in the west.

He began to think of the months he had spent in Buffalo Wallow; seeing Lorene Mowrey every day but, somehow, never quite realizing what she meant to him. Like a fool, he'd hung around Grace Loftus, who saw him not as a man at all but only as a means which might enable her to leave the place she despised and return East.

Now, anticipating his return, Casey closed his eyes, trying with quiet desperation to call to mind a clear picture of Lorene. But it always seemed to hang, blurred, at the far edge of his vision. It was like looking at her through frosted glass, her features shadowy and dim. . . .

He tried to conjure up images of the town's other inhabitants. Gooch, the telegraph operator, he saw clearly. Gooch, now dead . . . He envisioned Gooch's buxom wife . . . and Housman . . . Etheridge, and even Shawcross. . . .

He could see Grinstead's face, but not

Lorene's. . . .

Fear touched him, turned his spirit cold. Maybe it wasn't merely that he tried so hard; maybe there was another reason. Perhaps Moya had been back to Buffalo Wallow. Perhaps Lorene was already dead. . . .

He shook himself savagely. Slow to come out of his trance, he realized suddenly that his horse was tiring fast. Impatiently he urged him on, though he realized that the horse had only a few more miles in him. He hoped with grim desperation that he would pass a ranch or a homestead before the horse collapsed.

It wasn't likely. He had cut across country, forsaking roads and trails, traversing barren, unsettled land. He doubted that he'd see a living thing until he got to Buffalo Wallow. In the dark, he might even pass a ranch without seeing it. He couldn't force his tired mind to recall the location of the few ranches roundabout.

But he didn't slow down. If his horse gave out, he would walk. He would crawl if he had to, he told himself grimly. Suddenly it was of supreme importance for him to know that Lorene was all right. If she was, he'd turn the money over to her and then get back to Wagner's trail before it grew too cold.

The horse's head went down and he stumbled. Then his front quarters dropped, and Casey was catapulted over his head. He hit rolling, and struggled to his feet, dusty but unhurt.

The horse was done. He lay on his side, heaving, his eyes glassy.

Casey pulled his rifle from the boot. He removed his canteen and the saddle. Then he shot the horse. He felt a brief pang of pity for the abused brute.

He started walking, fast, leaving only the saddle behind. Dawn was becoming a fine gray line defining the eastern horizon. The air was cold and thin.

At last he topped a long rise of land and saw the wide flat before him, the town lying in its center like sediment left by evaporating water. He saw the wallow with its rim of dead cattails.

Suddenly he began to run, shamblingly.

Chapter 17

He ran until he was close to exhaustion, but still the town lay ahead like a mirage that receded as he traveled toward it.

The distance between him and the town

was still three to four miles, he knew. He couldn't run that far without killing himself. He slowed to a walk. He was panting heavily as he went on.

Dawn came; from deep gray, the sky gradually turned to pale blue. Ahead, dogs began to bark in the town. People were beginning to wake and stir.

Suddenly, Casey remembered the Pelton boy and the pinto horse. He was overcome with shame; this was the first time he'd thought of the boy's horse in all the time he had been away.

He hurried on. He would have to reach the town before its people were up and about, before they came outside. He kept the bulk of the boardinghouse between himself and the town. If observed, the approach of a man on foot would be bound to stir interest and curiosity.

He entered the town by the alley behind the boardinghouse, and sighed with relief. He had not been seen; he was sure of that.

He experienced a feeling of unreality, as though he'd never been away. No changes were apparent in the town. Everything seemed to be just as he had left it, except that now the way station corral was filled with horses, bickering over a mangerful of hay.

Casey was suddenly conscious of his own wild appearance, the rank, gamy smell of his unwashed body, and the heavy beard upon his face. He slipped along the alley and out to Main between two buildings. He looked across at Lorene Mowrey's shop, then up and down the street. A man came up the street, stopped at the telegraph office, unlocked the door and went inside.

If only that horse had stood up all the way to town! Now, this late, Casey was going to have trouble reaching Lorene and getting back out of town the same way, unseen. He had to have a horse and a saddle, and he should have them now so that if he was discovered he could leave in a hurry.

Another man came into the street from the way station and stopped to stretch and yawn and rub his eyes. Casey cursed under his breath, conscious of time passing fast, and turned back.

He entered the boardinghouse by the kitchen door. Grace Loftus was standing before the stove. Her forehead was damp and she was stirring a pot of oatmeal. Her eyes widened with sudden fear. There was no light of recognition in them.

Casey said, "Grace —"

"Casey?" she said, her tone incredulous; "Casey?"

He nodded and stared at her. He could not hold back the question, "Lorene — is she all right?"

"Of course," she said, looking at him sharply. "Why wouldn't she be?"

He felt his breath gust out with relief. He crossed the room, weak with it; he put his hands on Grace Loftus' shoulders and kissed her lightly. "You can't know how glad I am to hear that. I was afraid . . ."

She glanced fearfully toward the front door. "Casey, you've got to stay out of sight. There's a reward out for you! Didn't you know . . . ?"

He nodded. "I know, Grace," he said quietly.

"There's probably not a person in town that wouldn't turn you in for it."

He shook his head. "You wouldn't. Lorene wouldn't. Two people . . ." He looked at her in wonder.

"Casey, why did you come back? What do you want?"

He said, "I've got part of the money, almost a hundred thousand dollars. I wanted to turn it in. I thought Lorene . . ."

He could see how it hurt her, that he had thought of Lorene instead of her. She asked tightly, "Then what?"

"Then I'm going out again after Wagner

and Moya. I lost Wagner's trail a while back, but I can pick it up again. I know I can."

For a moment she was silent. He felt a nervous desire to be gone, to be moving, before everybody in town was up and about. He started to speak, but Grace interrupetd him, her tone desperate.

"Casey, give it up. You've done your part. Let Grinstead do the rest. I've got the boardinghouse sold, Casey. I'm going back East next week. Why don't you come with me? Come with me, Casey!"

He looked down at her and said gently, "I can't do it, Grace."

Her mouth tightened. "It isn't — just getting those men, is it? It's — Lorene?"

He nodded, and saw the flush stain her cheeks. Her eyes grew coldly angry. He turned away. At the door he stopped.

"Could you . . . ?" Then he shook his head. It wouldn't be fair to ask favors of Grace Loftus now. He said, "Nothing," and went outside.

He came to Main by the same route he'd used before and peered into the street. The same man was still down at its far end. He was faced the other way, watching a dog which was approaching him with its tail wagging.

Casey crossed the street, quickly and

nervously. He kept waiting for the dog to bark, but the dog must not have seen him.

He ducked between two buildings and crossed to Housman's back door. He knocked, and Marian Housman came to the door.

"Is your husband here?" he asked.

She didn't recognize him; she looked at him with ill-concealed distaste, then turned and called, "Matt!" Then she shut the door, leaving Casey outside. He wondered what he was worrying about. Nobody had recognized him so far.

But Matt Housman did. He came to the door, saw Casey, and quickly came outside, closing the door behind him.

"Casey! What in God's name are you doing here?"

"I need a horse. Can I take yours?"

"Sure, Casey, sure. Come on, I'll saddle him for you."

Casey Day knew gratitude then. No questions. No doubts. He must have built up one hell of a reputation in the past months, but Matt Housman acted just as he always had toward him.

He led the horse from the stable, thanked Housman humbly, and headed down the alley toward Lorene's shop. An excitement began to build in him, one he found it harder to control at every step he took. . . .

He knocked on the back door lightly. There was silence for a moment, then he heard light steps approaching. The door opened.

Her face was as white and pale as though she had somehow known it was he. He stepped toward her, putting out his hands.

"Lorene . . ."

Her eyes widened, and she took a backward step. Her head swung quickly to glance over her shoulder. Casey frowned, puzzled. Suddenly she rushed toward him, but she did not come to his arms; she pushed him violently out the door with a fiercely whispered, "Get out!," leaped back and slammed it behind her. He heard her sobbing through its panels, and heard a curse from a deep male voice.

"What the hell? Lorene . . . ?" He was ashamed of the thought before it had taken shape in his mind. He heard a sound like a slap behind the door and a child began to cry.

There was a shed behind the shop. He ran toward it and plunged inside, driven by a compulsion he did not understand himself.

His feeling that something was terribly wrong here became certainty when he saw the two horses, caked with sweat and dust, that stood at the manger calmly munching hay. Casey's heart suddenly felt like a ball of ice.

It wasn't possible! Wagner was miles away. And yet, who else would force his way into Lorene's shop? Who else could terrify her thus? Unless . . .

He heard the tinkle of breaking glass, and peered out the door of the shed. He heard Moya's voice call softly from the broken window in the rear of Lorene's shop. "Casey?"

Casey's heart leaped with savage exultation that faded instantly. Moya had Lorene at his mercy. Not only did he have her, but he had a child as well — maybe more than one. Lorene had probably taken in the Pelton kids, being the kind of person she was. . . .

So the pattern was repeating itself. Lorene was Moya's hostage, and Casey was helpless. Or was he? Wasn't there a difference now?

He called, "It's me, all right."

Moya's voice came again, "Come on in here with your hands in the air unless you want me to . . ." He left the sentence dangling.

Fury roared through Casey, fury that he controlled with difficulty. He made his voice evenly contemptuous. "Go to hell, Moya. I've got Bell's share of the stagecoach loot. You hear me? A hundred thousand dollars!"

His mind was racing. Moya's companion must be Wagner; it *had* to be Wagner! He remembered the man who had been with Wagner up on the pass. It hadn't been Moya. He'd have recognized Moya, even in driving snow, even at a distance. Then how . . . ? Wagner must have joined Moya somewhere after Casey had lost his trail. . . .

Moya called, "So?"

Casey said, throwing out his bait, "I'll toss it out on the ground, halfway between here and the back door." He hesitated then, considering the treachery of these men. But he knew he had no choice. The money wasn't sufficient bait. He had to offer himself too. He called, "Then I'll step out into the open. You can pick up the loot and come to the shed for your horses. You can ride away. I'll make no move to stop you."

"What if we gun you? What's to stop us?"

Casey said grimly, "You can try. And the gunshots will bring people running. They won't be as easy as they were before." He put into the statement a conviction he could not feel.

There was silence inside the shop. Casey could feel the tension building in his whole being. All the hardship and dangers of the past months were to come to nothing after all, he thought bitterly. In a few more minutes he'd be right back where he'd started. Or he'd be dead, and nothing accomplished. But he couldn't endanger Lorene or those kids. . . .

At last Moya called, "All right, Casey. You're on."

The door opened. Wagner stepped out first, a gun in his hand. Casey tossed the money belt into the yard, halfway between them. Then he stepped outside.

Moya followed Wagner out. Casey felt a wave of blinding hatred as he saw the man. It was all he could do to keep from reaching for his gun.

Moya came watchfully across the yard. Wagner followed. When they reached the worn money belt, they stopped.

Casey called, "Lorene? Are you all right?"

He heard her crying, probably with relief. But she stopped long enough to say, "Yes, Casey. Yes — we're all right!"

Casey said to Moya, "Pick it up, and get the hell out of here."

Moya picked up the money belt while Wagner covered Casey with his leveled gun. Casey kept waiting for the shot, for the smash of a bullet into his body. He swore that if they did shoot him, he'd get them both before he went out himself.

But Wagner didn't shoot. Moya straightened, looking at Casey. "I hear you killed Bell."

Casey said, "Buck, too."

Moya said without inflection, "You son-of-a-bitch."

Wagner said worriedly, "Let it go, for Christ's sake! Let's get out of here."

He caught Moya's arm and pulled him along toward Casey. Casey began to edge away.

Moya said wickedly, "That's right. Get out into the middle of the yard, you. I want you where we can see you." He studied Casey tensely, his eyes gleaming. "Shuck your gun, Casey."

Casey's heart sank. He'd hoped this wouldn't happen. Now he had a choice that must be made in seconds; he could draw and shoot it out with the pair, or he could shuck his gun and trust an honor he knew they didn't have.

He shrugged, and his hands went deliberatley to the buckle of his gun belt. He unfastened it watchfully and let gun and belt slide to the ground. Moya's eyes seemed to brighten.

Wagner said impatiently, "Get your horse,

Moya. Casey, you step away from your gun."

Casey stepped back. Moya smiled in evil fashion and sauntered deliberately toward the shed. He disappeared inside.

The tension in Casey became intolerable. He knew this was his most dangerous moment. Moya would try to kill him before he left; both Moya and Wagner would want him dead before they rode away.

And if they did kill him, he knew what Moya would do afterward. The man had an unholy lust for Lorene Mowrey. He'd get her, carry her away with him. . . .

Blood beat like a drum in Casey's temples. Moya came out of the shed leading one of the horses. He handed the reins to Wagner and returned to the shed without speaking.

Wagner swung to his saddle, his impatience to be gone very apparent. Casey glanced at his gun and belt lying on the ground a dozen feet from where he stood. He listened intently for sounds within the shed.

He heard nothing, and looked worriedly toward it.

A puff of powder smoke rolled from a wide crack in the shed wall. Casey felt the heavy bullet strike him.

He was spun clear around before he fell. His head felt as though it were floating a foot above his body. His mouth tasted the gritty dust of the yard and his ears heard Lorene screaming.

Numbed with shock, Casey clawed toward his gun and belt a dozen feet away. Dust from a second bullet showered over him. Scrambling crabwise, he reached the gun and tried to yank it clear of the holster.

It stuck. He dropped his chest down on the holster and pulled the gun clear.

Wagner was shooting at him from his dancing horse, missing because of the horse's movement. Casey couldn't see Moya for a moment. Then he saw the man ride out of the shed's doorway.

Rolling onto his back, Casey flung a shot at him. He missed, but Moya's horse was hit in the neck. The horse went down and catapulted Moya over his head.

Casey sat up and steadied the wobbly gun on his knees. He aimed at Moya's rolling body and squeezed off another shot.

He missed again. Moya got up and began to run.

Wagner swung around, spurred toward Moya and helped him swing up behind him. Casey fired at the pair and saw dust puff from Wagner's left sleeve.

Casey got to his feet, surprised that he could stand. His left arm hung like a rag from his shoulder. He could feel the warmth of blood on it, was dimly aware that blood was dripping from his fingers.

But he could stand; he could ride and he could shoot.

Housman's horse stood in the alley behind the shed where Casey had left him. Casey ran toward him and climbed awkwardly into the saddle.

Wagner and Moya, riding their single horse, had cut through toward Main and were heading for the way-station corral. They had to have two horses if they were going to get away.

Casey heard a rifle boom, and then he saw Housman kneeling, firing at the fleeing pair. Moya turned and threw a shot, and Housman slumped over and lay still.

Casey spurred after them, through a weed-grown vacant lot. He saw a crowd that was beginning to gather on Main Street, and discerned the burly shape of Shawcross running from the boardinghouse, a shotgun in his hands.

The shotgun roared, and the shot pelted Casey and his horse like a stinging hail. He thanked God the range was what it was, and that Shawcross' loads were birdshot instead of buck. The shotgun roared again, and again the shot pelted Casey. The pain of it, added to that pounding in his limply dangling arm, was almost more than he could stand.

He swung to follow Moya and Wagner, hopeful now for the first time. He'd catch them when they stopped at the corral, if Shawcross didn't close the range and get him first. Shawcross, running, was stuffing more shells into the breech of the shotgun.

Suddenly, from a corner of his eye, Casey saw a small form come running from the door of Lorene's shop. It was Tony Pelton, grown bigger since Casey had last seen him, but still a small boy for the job he obviously was set on doing.

He flung himself at Shawcross' legs and wrapped his arms around them. Shawcross went to the ground heavily. The fool probably hadn't realized he was helping Wagner and Moya by shooting at Casey. He'd jumped to the conclusion that the three were together. Or maybe he didn't care. Maybe that reward was the only thing in his mind.

Casey, in spite of the pain in his arm, felt grimly elated. Wagner and Moya could have ridden out, free, with the money in their hands. But Moya had had to try to kill Casey, and now his treachery had put the pair of them in a spot.

He saw Moya fling himself from the horse at the way-station corral gate. Pounding along, he saw Wagner look over his shoulder. Then Wagner turned his horse and began to fire at Casey. He got off one shot, then began frantically reloading.

A horse, probably that of the new way-station operator, was standing, saddled, inside the corral. Moya ran toward it and vaulted to the saddle. He whirled the horse and spurred toward the open gate. He lifted his gun to fire at Casey, now no more than twenty yards away.

Casey lifted his gun barrel, letting go the reins of his horse. At eye level, he steadied the gun and looked at Moya's chest above its sights. He fired.

Moya's throat fountained blood as the bullet tore into it. His horse came through the gate, terrified, and spilled the outlaw's body from the saddle as he turned. He swung directly into Casey's unguided horse and collided with him violently. Casey was thrown from his saddle, over the other horse's back and onto the ground beyond.

The fall knocked the wind out of him, but he doggedly rolled onto his side. His gun was still in his hand. He lifted it stubbornly.

Wagner whirled his horse, ready to line him out and away, but Casey's bullet took him through the body before he could complete the turn. He fell from the saddle, but his right boot caught in the stirrup and would not come loose. The horse, frantic with fear, galloped away, dragging Wagner, head down, along the dry and rutted street.

Lorene Mowrey came running then, and a strange and foolish pride brought Casey to his feet, all the pain and the weakness and the dizziness forgotten for the moment. He shoved his gun into his belt on his second attempt and laid his right arm around her shoulders, letting her bear some of his weight now that his moment of exhilaration was passing. . . .

She was just as he remembered her, except that Moya had put a kind of breathless terror in her. But that began to leave her face as soon as he touched her.

She began to cry, and her tears were warm and soft against Casey's cheek. The three Pelton kids came, in solemn single file, and stood looking at him with shy bashfulness.

Matt Housman came limping along toward him from the vacant lot where he had fallen. Casey stared at him and breathed a sigh of relief. Housman grinned painfully, "Just a flesh wound in the leg, Casey. I'll live."

Casey felt weakness flooding him now. He

said, "The money's on them — all of it that's left. Will you — see that it gets into the way-station safe — and wire Grinstead?"

Housman nodded. Lorene drew Casey toward her shop. "Darling, darling, let's get that arm taken care of."

They were all around him then, the people of the town. They were helping him, smiling at him and praising him.

In his dazed and weakened state, it became suddenly inordinately important to Casey that he understand how Wagner and Moya had happened to be here. He stopped, and looked down at Lorene.

She must have known the question that was forming in his mind, for she said with a shudder, "Moya came after me, early this morning before it was light. Then Wagner showed up, and when he said you were trailing him, Moya figured you'd be along soon. They knew you'd killed Bell and Moya guessed you'd have Bell's share of the money with you."

"Then it wasn't Moya that was with Wagner up in the mountains. I didn't think it was."

She said, "I heard Wagner say someone else had been with him. The man got frightened when he found out who you were and what was involved. He slipped away the night before last while Wagner was asleep."

"But how did Wagner know Moya was coming here?"

She shuddered again involuntarily. "He knew where Moya was hiding out, I think. When he got there and found Moya gone, he must have remembered that Moya had wanted to take me along when they left here before. . . ."

Casey said gently, "Don't talk about it, Lorene. Don't even think about it any more. It's over."

Yes, it was over. All the weariness of the long months was not a heaviness within his mind and body. He was glad that the people of Buffalo Wallow felt the way they did about him. But mostly he was glad that his job was done. The chase was over; the pursuit was ended. For him now there was only rest. And Lorene . . .

He smiled down into her tear-dimmed eyes. Tomorrow, all the days of his life, he would be with Lorene. Life could offer little more to any man.

We hope you have enjoyed this Large Print book. Other Thorndike, Wheeler, and Chivers Press Large Print books are available at your library or directly from the publishers.

For information about current and upcoming titles, please call or write, without obligation, to:

Publisher
Thorndike Press
295 Kennedy Memorial Drive
Waterville, ME 04901
Tel. (800) 223-1244

or visit our Web site at:

www.gale.com/thorndike
www.gale.com/wheeler

OR

Chivers Large Print
published by BBC Audiobooks Ltd
St James House, The Square
Lower Bristol Road
Bath BA2 3SB
England
Tel. +44(0) 800 136919
email: bbcaudiobooks@bbc.co.uk
www.bbcaudiobooks.co.uk

All our Large Print titles are designed for easy reading, and all our books are made to last.